# On Both Sides of the Midline

## Jacob Gindin

Senior Editors & Producers: Contento
Translation to English: Shalom Goldman
Editor: Judith Deborah Levy
Illustrations: "Persons" by Chaim Topol
Cover and Book Design: Liliya Lev Ari
Producer: Rinat Maya

Book (Hebrew) published in Israel by Zmora-Bitan, 1999

ISBN: 978-965-550-589-4

International sole distributor: Contento
22 Isserles Street, 6701457 Tel Aviv, Israel
www.ContentoNow.com
Netanel@contento-publishing.com

# On Both Sides of the Midline

## Jacob Gindin

# About the translator

 Shalom Goldman is professor of religion at Middlebury College in the USA.

He is the author, editor and co-author of six books, including "Zeal for Zion: Christians, Jews and the Idea of the Promised Land". Among his arts projects is the libretto of Philip Glass's opera "Akhnaten". His most recent book is "Jewish-Christian Difference and Modern Jewish Identity". (2015)

# Gindin thanks Topol

Chaim Topol is a world famous stage and cinema performer, and the ikon who was made by "Fiddler on the Roof" - one of the most successful films ever. Topol made over 25 films and produced 10. As a theatre actor appeared in the West end in London and on Broadway in N.Y. among other stages in the U.S. and Canada, the U.K., Australia Japan and Israel. Topol – winner of many awards, among them: For **best actor** – the "Golden Gate", Two Golden Globes, the Donatello - Italy, and San Sebastian, and so for stage awards in New York, London, Sidney, Tel Aviv etc.

Topol is a gifted illustrator who has been drawing mainly portraits. Topol has illustrated over 30 books including three written by himself. His illustrations keep being exhibited in galleries and institutions.

After reading the manuscript of on both sides of Midline Topol found it "a pleasure" to illustrate the book, to match some illustrations of his "Persons" to the spirit of the book. Chaim Topol is founder of the Society of Friends of interRAI, and supported the young interRAI scholars grants to which this book will contribute.

# Table of Contents

CHAPTER 1:

# Weakness

*B*efore the anesthetist went into action, and while the surgeon was having his surgical gloves put on, Yitzhak thought of his sister, who never woke up from a chest operation.

"Goodbye, goodbye," he whispered. No one heard him. His eyes got heavy. "Maybe we'll see each other again." Almost a month had passed since he was snared by God's net and transformed into some other being. Someone was fiddling with his arm, with the green valve on the IV tubing that was stuck in his skin.

In the beginning, when it all happened, Yitzhak knew that it was morning. He woke up to the sound of dishes rattling as Malka worked in the kitchen to the left, along a small hallway–just three meters long and then a right into the kingdom of cooking pots and frying pans, a place always filled with a mix of sounds and sighs, the gurgling of running water, knives and forks clanging in the sink, the slurping of tasting, the sound of the knife on the cutting board as vegetables were thinly sliced. He knew how to tell the difference between the creaking of the cabinet above the sink and that of the cabinet below it–and could distinguish between the sound of the milk silverware drawer and that of the meat silverware. Even the whisper of the door of the large refrigerator was different from that of the door of the freezer. He caught the smell of coffee and cardamom and saw in his mind's eye the foam on top of a cup of coffee, a cup whose octagonal base was narrower than its round mouth. He knew too that today was Sunday. Over the forty-four years they had been together, Malka woke him every Sunday with coffee in bed. Yitzhak returned the favor on Friday afternoons, at exactly five p.m., standing above her with a glass of lemonade when she woke up from her nap. Even on those Friday afternoons in which there arose in the arguments and whimpers in their spacious apartment–and Malka ran around to contain the shame with the plastic shutters on their aluminum frame so the neighbors wouldn't hear them in the courtyard– a haze of rest and quiet eventually settled over the house when Malka lay down for her Friday nap. It always ended with a lemonade awakening, Yitzhak standing over her with a glass saucer that held a rattling cup–the result of a slight tremor that he had developed since the bar mitzvah of Eitan, the grandson who grew up in America–and on the cup was a slice of lemon wedged on both sides of the glass.

"Malka," he would whisper and at once she was awake and sitting up, the glass in her hand, and she was waiting to see the moistness in his eyes. Forty-four years. Sometimes she pretended that she was still asleep, offering him her left shoulder so that he would shake it and wake her up.

On the day it started, as she stood by his bed and clanged the spoon against the glass again, the sharp smell of Sunday assailing his nostrils, he understood that his eyes were closed. He always greeted Malka with his eyes open, sitting up in bed with the blanket pulled over his chest and the giant pillow supporting his back. Now he was on his back, his arms under the covers. He opened his mouth, closed it again, moved his lips and then did it again.

"What's wrong with you, Itzhak?" Her voice trembled.

He tried to open his eyes and look at her. His arm jutted out of the cave of the covers toward her, and his hand touched her apron, then sank in a vertical motion. It stayed there limp, blocking half the distance between the bed and the closet. His hand, palm down, was sturdy and rough from fifty years of carpentry. The scar from his work accident–from when he was working for the Army–had turned white. Without thinking about it, Malka used to run her finger over the scar while they were watching television.

Now he opened his eyes, smiled, clutched her hand to his chest, and dropped his eyes again. "Another hour's sleep won't hurt me today," he whispered. He turned over to his left side–not all at once, but in stages–first his head, then his right arm. He stabbed his fingertips into the border of the mattress, beyond which everything descended to the cold floor below.

He tried bending arm and forearm against each other at the axis of his elbow. Somehow he managed to raise his shoulder slightly. A tremor ran across his back, between his shoulder blades, and his armpit stretched open, thin-haired–a seam was open along a line rising up from the waist. His shoulder rose for a moment, hesitant, afraid it would fall off onto the sheet. The pit of his arm closed again–almost. But no, the shoulder stopped in the middle of its journey, unable to complete its task, and back on the same route almost to the point from which it had started to rise, and Yitzhak was like a bystander watching it fall, but no, here it was, pulling itself up again, the shoulder wouldn't give up - if it drowned it would die, and the eyes sought help, crying out to this stupid left side, and then suddenly came the leg. His right leg, still underneath the covers, hadn't sensed the hopelessness of the shoulder on the same side.

On its own, through its own power, his leg pushed and came between the blanket and the left leg, the one stuck to the sheets. It moved a bit and fell back not far from where it had started. And now came his pelvis, pulling along with it his butt and his waist, and it came down, collapsing with it that whole side of his body, the whole line from his shoulder and down through his ribs; all of his body came tumbling down without control or plan, and Yitzhak ended up turned over and twisted, with his face on the pillow, and the whole effort was too much. Who had declared this idiotic war and what for? And how is it that his body has collapsed? And how the hell did he find his corpse in the rubble? He pushed with the arm and leg whose importance he already recognized, straightened himself out, and smiled at Malka. "I can't get up." And before she put her hand under the covers to cup his heel with her palms, she placed the glass down on the dresser, bent her knees and her trunk and stretched sideways, like a trapeze artist, to the left and the right. Pulling his heel and rocking from side to side, she cried, "Alarm clock, alarm clock!" Yitzhak gave her a tight smile. He bit his lower lip, stretched his neck, raised his head a bit off the pillow, and gingerly let it fall back, as if it were a fragile object. "When was the last time you were my alarm clock?" he whispered.

She remembered that it had been at the Dead Sea, maybe three or four years ago. They went there with his sister and her husband. The holiday was a gift in honor of their golden wedding anniversary.

"Maybe if you took my blanket off first," he said. He made a chewing motion twice with his empty mouth. He looked paler than ever to her. Malka felt the blood leave her face; she was sinking, sinking. She leaned back and felt the cool of the morning in the Formica paneling on the closet at her back. She searched, as if blind, for the edge of the bed, sat down on its edge with half of her thigh and butt perched there, and pushed against Yitzhak's knee, which she found under her. Realizing this she moved right, but then again fell against his knee with all her weight. She hesitated for a moment and then suddenly regained her strength. Straightening herself out she put her arms out to him, and Yitzhak, as if swept up by her determination, put out his right arm, grabbed on to her, and tried with all his might to sit up straight. At the end of that effort she had to pull him by the arm so that he could complete his rise. When he was two-thirds of the way up, she put her right hand on his neck and pulled him to her pelvis. Once he used to cling there on his own power and with tenderness.She had to hold him to her, so that he wouldn't drag her down with him. What if she lost her balance suddenly, while she was holding him? Overcome with the understanding that he was completely dependent on her, she trembled. For a moment he regained his balance and her grip loosened. She saw the fear in his eyes, saw his brow furrow. And while she gazed at him he slipped from her grip, and even though she let him fall she fell with him on to the covers, her breasts crushed painfully against his chest. Then came belly and thighs, and neck and head, and at the end all the weight. She was falling on him, falling and falling, plummeting from the height of a mountain down to a dark abyss, falling endlessly.

As if possessed she yelled: "Idiot, enough already. Stop this stupidity. What can you be thinking?" Still lying down she pushed him off her. "Can't you see that I've been on my feet since early this morning? Look at my veins, they are blue as grapes." She got up heavily and turned away from him. "Go get your own coffee!" She stormed into the kitchen, bumping against the walls of the hallway, her slippers banging against the floor, as if her feet had forgotten how normal people walk. She grabbed the edge of the sink and dabbed her face with the yellow rag. It was still damp from when she had used it to sponge down the counter. She stuffed the rag in her mouth and choked her cries with it. She was breathing heavily through her nostrils (it sounded like a tired steam engine), and she knew that Yitzhak was listening to her and seeing her. A feeling that ants were crawling on her tingled up her fingers. The wall phone was watching her, right in front of her face. She hit the 6 key. After what seemed an eternity of rings, she heard a whirring sound and knew that he had already left for work. The answering machine picked up, goddammit. She slammed down the phone, took the rag out of her mouth, fished a slice of lemon out of a plastic container, and began to chew on it.

At the carpentry shop, Salim the Arab worker said that Herzl had not yet come in this morning. She left a message that he should get in touch.

Malka made herself a cup of hot lemonade and placed it on the tray with some low-fat cheese and thin crackers.

When the doorbell rang she was sitting on the recliner in the living room. She had almost finished the cheese but hadn't yet touched the hot drink. Her stare was fixed; not noticing the heavily framed tapestry that her sister had given her sixteen years ago, when they had moved into the house. In the picture a noble horse with an outstretched neck reared up on its legs against a background of delicate clouds. When she didn't hear any answer, Aviva, "the most hypocritical and audacious of daughters-in-laws" opened the door and pushed Guy into the apartment, knocking the metal door behind her. "Malka, the nose-drops are in his pocket." Guy ran into the apartment and disappeared from her sight.

In front of her she saw the red light of the hot water heater. "Hello, what's going on? Anyone home?"

Aviva closed the door silently and went into the kitchen. She noted the dirty yellow rag on the kitchen floor yellow. and stopped. "Guy, come right away to mommy, sweetie." Her voice rose, broke, and shook. On the sink there was a large economy bottle of cleaning fluid, a white swan sailing on its blue label. From the street she could hear the prolonged honking of a hoarse car. The sound of running water from a neighboring apartment came to her. She heard the voice of her eldest child: "Grandma, see how I can wipe my nose. Here, in the handkerchief, see." The whoosh of his nostrils went into the tissue paper. In the living room she found Malka hiding a mute cry, trembling powerfully into Guy's shoulder while the child was still puffing into the snot-filled Kleenex.

The routine appearance of Guy and Aviva brought Malka back. To Aviva she said: "Go see Grandpa, in the bedroom." She pointed her chin in his direction. She got up from her chair. "Come," she stood up,"let's go together," she said, smiling. "I don't know what happened to me, why I'm acting like a robot. Look how I gobbled down all of this cheese, like a slob." She couldn't believe that she could be so happy to see Aviva; she always took Herzl to her own parent's house on the night of the Seder and she joked about Malka's hot lemonade: "Grandma's coffee," she called it. Her work alwways came before the children–she never missed a day. Malka knew, but never told anyone, that Herzl, "the best-looking" of her children,deserved a better wife.And the stupid one got angry when she tried to tell him, before the kids were born, that Aviva was no Penina Rosenblum. Since then she hadn't raised the subject, and Herzl seemed less and less like himself, like when he came back from the army during the war in Lebanon. It was then that Yitzhak quipped, "Goodbye (Shalom) to Herzl, instead of Peace (Shalom) to the Galilee."

Yitzhak was sitting up in their bed on her side. The blanket from his side of the bed lay defeated on the floor, on top of the hairy throw rug. The coffee was far away and untasted; it had moved away from the saucer. The cup's journey to the edge of the night table was marked by coffee stains. Aviva smelled something odd. She still hadn't understood what had happened to Yitzhak and laughed at him from a distance. "Say good morning to grandpa!" she said to Guy. That way she didn't have to look directly at Yitzhak. She always spoke to him by way of the children, and now she continued to stare at Guy intently even after he spoke to his grandfather.

"I'm late, see you later. Bye, Guy sweetie, be a good boy." She went out into the kitchen, and Malka could hear her as she dialed the phone. The line was silent for a moment. "Salim, give me Herzl, quickly." Again there was silence. Guy moved closer to Yitzhak, stood facing him, and scrutinized him. Aviva's voice could be heard from the kitchen: "Herzl, come home to your Mama. Something bad happened this morning, and Guy is with her. Maybe you can take him to the carpentry shop. I'll be free by this afternoon." Then her tone softened and got sweeter. "Me too, Herzl." "Herzl will be here in about two hours." She tossed this remark over her shoulder as she walked out, her shoes making no sound on the floor.

Yitzhak sat bent over with the weight of twenty extra years. He was staring at Guy's belly. The white sheet was stained with the outlines of a new, spreading continent, something like the unbroken coastline of Africa; and his pajama pants in the front were also stained, down to mid-thigh, their light blue color turned dark with urine–the left side was even more soaked.

"I called you, but I couldn't hold it in." He gave a humble smile. "Guy, go wait a minute in the living room." He caressed his grandson's back with just one finger. He looked at the wondering child and signaled with his eyes toward the door. "It's nothing, grandpa just wants to straighten himself out."

Dr. Sovrin arrived out of breath, not long after Malka left a message for her with Sigal the secretary, whose voice chewed gum. On the holidays on Passover, Shavuot, and also on the doctor's birthday, Malka remembered to visit the doctor and bring her a box of chocolates. Over the years a supermarket friendship developed between them. A couple of times their shopping carts met. "So how are the kids?" or "Where did you find that kind of flour?" She was a good-looking woman, well-dressed, and she displayed good taste. Her perfume was subtle, a silk scarf was wound around her neck, its ends bound together by a silver pin. Her wide feet seemed to contradict her calm face, and her laced-up leather shoes seemed too small for those big ankles.

"Whenever you need the elevator, it's busy. It seems that Segal is again changing tenants."

Even though the kupat cholim (HMO clinic) was two blocks away, it seemed that Dr. Sovrin lived in all the apartments in the neighborhood; she had lightness, eagerness, and cheer sufficient for them all. "Let's have a look at Yitzhak." She put down her masculine-looking dark bag and pulled out a stethoscope. "We'll check on what's happening to your grandfather." She ruffled Guy's hair, and filled the room with confidence. Malka took advantage of the moment, before the feeling dissipated, and opened the window.

"You're a little pale, Yitzhak. When's the last time we had a blood test?" she looked directly at him. "Say aaah! Open your mouth, now." She bent over, peering into his barely open mouth." "Open it a little more, please." She straightened herself out. "The throat is O.K." From her bag she pulled out a blood pressure cuff; two rubber tubes hung down from it, a clock-face dial on one tube, and a rubber balloon on the other–they were dancing and shaking one against the other. The smell of urine hung over the room. It was diluted by the street air that came in through the window, fluttering the white lace curtain. While the doctor was getting ready, Malka rolled Yitzhak back into bed and helped him take off his pajamas pants. It wasn't easy. She had to pull on them again and again, until her back hurt. When they were free, she let them drop heavily on the sheet. Yitzhak's testicles seemed to have lengthened and become flaccid–they seemed redder and tougher than what she was acquainted with. For forty-four years the sight of his balls had excited her–but not today. "Oy vey," she said; it just fell out of her mouth. Then she rolled him over, like a sack, to his side of the bed, and tore off the sheet from her half of the mattress. "Why did you have to go and soil *my* side of the bed?" As soon as she said it she regretted it. She stood up straight to look at him; it was as if she hadn't spoken a word, his face a blank to her. Frightened, she bit her lower lip till it hurt.

Dr.Sovrin was busy around Yitzhak's upper arm. She wound the cuff, pulling his lower arm to the right. "Help me a little more, please." When she was angry, even a little angry, her French accent was more pronounced, and her voice more assertive.

"Excuse me, Doctor, really, excuse me." Yitzhak tried to help. Malka ran out of the room; covering her mouth with her hand and pulling Guy by the collar of his ninja shirt. "Let's watch TV. There are lots of good programs on in the morning." She looked around for a moment. "Let's use the remote control." She pressed it and noise came out of the TV, followed by a dance of dots.

When she returned to the bedroom Dr. Sovrin had her marvelous smile on. "Blood pressure is excellent." From the living room came a loud conversation in English. "Excuse me for a moment." By the time she walked into the living room the child had changed stations. "Guy, my love, did your your mother give you breakfast?" The child responded vigorously, making her happy with his sweet impish look, as if he knew that this was the thing to do right here and now. Quickly she held his head in her hands and kissed him in the middle of his head, right at the spot his hair fountained from. She noticed that he was smiling–it was a child's smile of victory. Using the remote she turned down the sound and went back to Yitzhak.

Dr. Sovrin, the stethoscope in her ears, leaned over Yitzhak and placed the metal button over his heart. Malka remembered that that was where she used to rest her head, exactly at that place. She wondered if Yitzhak, absorbed in his examination, was aware that her old feeling of jealousy was awakened. "What a rotten emotion." For years it had been nibbling away at her happiness and satisfaction.

The doctor moved the instrument up–almost to the base of his neck, and then moved down, to the left and even further down, down to his blind nipple, and on further, making her way through the grey hair of his chest, advancing according to some hidden plan.

"What is she listening to for so long?" she thought to herself. "Heart's O.K.," the doctor announced. "Is something hurting you, Mr. Yitzhak, your head, your stomach, something?" He shook his head to say no, and added, "No, nothing hurts me." Malka could hardly hear his voice, and she added, "No, nothing hurts him. Yitzhak doesn't have pains. He never complains. Even when he had that abscess in his toe. Remember?"

Dr. Sovrin turned to Yitzhak. "Why do you close your eyes when you talk to me? You don't want to see me?" Yitzhak opened them wide, questioning. The furrows in his brow, his cheeks, his eyebrows were all mobilized in the effort. Stretching out his eyelids from both sides, he said, "Doctor, I don't know what's come over me, I'm like a dishrag. I can't stand up, can't sit down, can't even hold this little glass." His voice was weak, but steady and clear.

Malka pointed to the glass, cold and without its saucer, on the dresser. "There it is. He even spilled a little and made a mess for me." His face fell, and his brown eyes shuttered down yet again. "Lift your leg, please." The doctor picked up the blanket all at once, and tossed it on to the stripped side of the bed. Naked from the waist down, Yitzhak bent one leg. He dragged his heel up the bed toward his body. The knee rose, its kneecap swallowed and sunken into the dome of the joint. His leg almost reached the back of his thigh. Then he pulled his other leg up, this one more slowly, as he did battle with a fold in the sheet that blocked the legs' path. He did it. "Here, I made it."

"Now lift your right leg please," ordered Doctor Sovrin. Yitzhak went to work. You could see that the effort was taking concentration and planning. First he spread the fingers of both hands, making sure that each finger knew what it had to do, like a pianist about to attack the keyboard. Then, sure of their grip, he thrust out his arms, and with them his shoulders. The arch of his left foot pressed into the mattress. From the bed, his three extremities sticking out, his right leg was as if electrified with the message sent to it. It trembled slightly, and the whole weight of it, from the heel to the toes, lifted up from its resting place, moving along with it the foot and thigh, which had been stuck together.

And while the distal part of his leg hung in the air, Yitzhak slowly brought his thigh to his chest, and his leg hung folded up from behind, like a pelican's beak on its neck. When the leg rested on his stomach, the tension in his fingers relaxed slowly, and the trembling caused by all of the effort lessened, though it didn't disappear completely, and the pads of his fingers returned and curled over the sheet, like a buoy of a diver. From this point on he put his effort into raising his leg. It lay prone on his thigh, which had folded itself on his belly–and so it was thigh on leg on belly, like three stories of an apartment house that had collapsed in an earthquake, that Malka saw on television. Yitzhak entered the last stage, and the leg got heavier. He tried, pushing and squeezing, and a great fart escaped from his exposed behind, which curved without shame and without honor directly in front of where Malka was standing. During the whole physical exam Malka stood hugging her breasts, leaning against the laundry closet across from the bed, and of everything that happened in the room, she saw only his shame, it was dark red, hanging between his legs, and she couldn't recognize in it the thing that she had kneaded with her hands–over the past forty-four years–to make it hard. The fart signaled to Yitzhak that the whole game was impossible. And without straightening the leg which had sunk into him and made his breathing difficult he turned himself to his left side and the weight of his leg and its thigh dragged the back after it to the side.

Malka attacked the exposed half of the mattress and spread the blanket to cover his nakedness. She lifted the blanket and hurried to improve her job of covering him, taking care to pull each corner of the blanket to its place. Out of the corner of her eye she saw Guy standing in the doorway and understood that he had seen everything. "Get out of here, and go to the living room immediately, or else I'll call to get your mom from work."

Dr.Sovrin put the stethoscope in her bag and then locked it with its brass clasp. "If this continues tomorrow we will do something. It's not good." She checked to make sure that the bag was really closed. "I have to go back to the office. Send your son; I'll write him a referral to the emergency room. If, God forbid, it gets worse," she said with the same smile on her face, "we will send him right away. I have a long list of patients waiting." She looked at him. "As soon as I heard it was Yitzhak, I dropped everything and came over without giving it a thought. Meanwhile–drink a lot, with sugar and lemon, please."

"You're still at the door." Malka chastised Guy in a low and evil voice. The child didn't move.

The doctor swung her bag. "Mrs. Malka, leave the boy alone now. Did you understand me?"

"What's there to understand," she murmured, "he's already pissed in the bed like an infant. What could be any worse?" She herself was shocked by her question, and its audacity.

"Oh, you don't know. It could be so much worse that you'll miss today. And," she added quickly, "all of this, Mr. Yitzhak, is theoretical; it doesn't have to do with you. Please don't worry–I have to calm down the Mrs. for the grandchild's sake. The boy really is sweet."

Malka made tea with lemon and found drinking straws in the grandkids' drawer in the kitchen. These were wide straws, the kind you could bend at an angle. She put it all on a tray and placed it in front of Yitzhak, right close to him. She stuck the tip of the straw in the corner of his mouth and his cheeks sank as he made a sucking motion, bringing up big sips through the pipe.

"There's honey in it. " He smiled the way he used to.

Herzl opened the door with his own key. He did not ring the bell. "Guy, where are you, Daddy has already wasted part of the morning." He walked into the living room. "What's up, Guy?" He patted the child's shoulder. "Taking care of Grandpa, huh?" Guy didn't respond and kept watching the morning kids' program. "I'm going to make myself some coffee." He walked back toward the kitchen and stopped in the doorway of the bedroom. Herzl was a big man–wide and tall, he had a broad forehead and laugh lines fixed in the corner of his eyes. Dark blue work clothes were his regular outfit. He would take them off and shower only after reading the newspaper, talking to the child and checking his school notebooks. For a long time he worshipped the ground his Aviva walked on, and the greater his love for her, the more his mother hated her daughter-in-law. "You found someone with a big mouth," she complained.

Standing at the door he realized that something had changed in the house. "Come here," his mother said to him, "Dad has become a dishrag. He pees in bed, can't sit up. The doctor was just here." Herzl stared at her, wondering what to say.

"Go have some coffee. Meanwhile I'll finish up with dad." He obeyed. In the shower he washed his hands with soap. The sharp smell of ammonia rose up from the sheet and pajamas pants that were in the sink. But he didn't go to the kitchen; he retraced his steps. Malka sat next to Yitzhak and ran her finger through his hair. Despite his age he hadn't gone bald. "Get up for a minute, Mom," he said. He bent down on his knees and put his large hand under his father's head. Malka didn't follow while Herzl brought his father up to a bent-over flaccid sitting position. "Go bring a chair," he ordered. She dragged a chair from the dining corner and muttered, "Look at you, big hero, giving orders to your mother." She pointed toward the living room with her head. Herzl threw her a look. Then, with one hand he put the chair on the bed, its four legs pointing toward the wall, shoved a pillow between the seat and Yitzhak, and moved the support closer to his father's back.

Yitzhak smiled at his son's practical move. He hadn't made a mistake when he passed the carpentry shop to Herzl and thus angered Jonathan, Malka's favorite, who then picked himself up and went to America. "What's going on, Dad?" Herzl asked satisfied with himself.

"I don't have the strength to live another hour." Yitzhak pointed with his head toward heaven. "I'm like the tin after you put it in the oven." Of all his children, Herzl, the eldest, was the only one he called by his name when they were talking.

"I saw you the day before yesterday, while I was in the van on the way to the bus station," Herzl said. "You could hardly drag your feet around. I thought maybe you were wearing new shoes." He pointed with his finger to the soles of his feet. "In the evening I even talked to Aviva about it, that it looked strange, how you were dragging yourself around." Herzl looked at his mother.

"Very nice! Talking to Aviva about your dad. I'm sure it touched her heart. I'm sure she didn't sleep all night," Malka hissed. "And what about the phone? Did the phone company cut you off? Why didn't you call to find out if your father was alive?"

Yitzhak lifted his hand and then put it down. "Do me a favor, leave the child alone. What is this foolishness?" Herzl ignored them and went on talking. "You should have continued to come to the carpentry shop. I said to ..." He stopped. "You shouldn't be without work. That will finish you off. Just get some of your strength back, and I'll bring you back into the shop, into your room, your table. You'll see how you'll turn into a lion, you'll see."

"Stop chattering. It's now three days that he hasn't been able to take down the garbage. I didn't say a word, took it down myself. Aviva won't come and help me take anything down, unless it's my shroud. Now–go make some coffee, for him too," and she added, "What's this talk of going back to the carpentry shop? "

# CHAPTER 2:

# Yitzhak

A uniformed guard stood at the entrance to the hospital. He let in all cars that had stickers, as well as cars whose owners could convince him that their tormented passengers couldn't make it on foot. These, and only these, were admitted to the much-desired lot in front of the emergency room. To the guard Herzl pointed at his father Yitzhak, who was splayed out on the worn-out and dirty upholstery of the back seat; his head was supported by a white pillow, white with rose colored flowers that Malka had taken from their bed.

Acting out of dire necessity, and without waiting for permission, Herzl advanced forward. To his mother's pride he parked the car at the very entrance to the building. "I'm here to take my father to the ER," he said to the large uniformed fellow who stood there. Only then did the fellow, who looked a bit apologetic, offer to help.

"The only way I'm going into the hospital is on my own two feet," said Yitzhak. "Do you see that fence behind the electric pole? The one they painted green?" He was pointing to the fence, while supporting his arm on the headrest of the front seat. "I made that fence, back when the director of the hospital was the fellow married to the tall woman from the book store." He talked to Herzl, who in the meanwhile had grabbed him by the arms, near his shoulders, so that at this point he felt his fingers moistening from the sweat in his father's armpits. "When I used to come through the gate, all the janitors would do me honor. That was back when people valued work well done."

For a moment Herzl felt his father slipping away from him, felt that even though he couldn't carry his own weight, his knees soft and bending, his father was reluctant, as if it wasn't him that would go crashing to the pavement.

He held on tighter to his father's arms–damn sticks–they didn't cooperate, just stuck out and flapped at his sides. At this point Herzl had no choice but to support Yitzhak with his legs. He pushed his father's knees back toward the car, and was able to accomplish this by pressing his thigh against them. It was clear to both of them that Yitzhak would not make it on his own to the nearby wheelchair, which was deserted at moderate distance in the entrance hall, near the security guard, who was checking people's bags.

Herzl rearranged his dad and carried him before him on outstretched arms, arms at a right angle, and carried him in front of him, like a salesman in a fine men's clothing store, displaying a bolt of cloth to a discerning customer. Patients, and those who accompanied them to the hospital, sat in the entrance area. Only one middle-aged man, a few days' stubble on his face, stretched out on a bench that he had conquered.

An old woman with a high-pitched voice was keening in a Yemenite accent, "Whyillii, whyillii, yaammaaa." A young man in rubber thongs and a filthy T-shirt was skipping across the space on one foot. His eyes had an amused look, and the sore on his foot was encrusted with blood.

Yitzhak closed his eyes so that he wouldn't see himself embarrassed in public, carried and humiliated along the length of the hall. Someone in a uniform hastened to open for them a glass door that was framed in aluminum.

The sour smell of illness hit his nostrils. The place was a beehive of activity, of people dressed in white or green humming here and there. They were all busying themselves with those people who were not in any uniform dress, people who were simply standing in one place, or who had no idea where they were or where they should turn. Very few people spoke, their voices drowned out by the unintelligible screams of a male patient and the constant and rapid regular digital chatter of a monitor.

"First name, family name, father's name, date of birth," was fired at them by the receptionist at the counter. Malka replied hesitantly.

"Lady, it doesn't help me if you give the Hebrew date of birth." The receptionist cut her off.

"But," said Malka, "that's the way we celebrate birthdays, all happy occasions in fact, and also ..."

"Excuse me for saying so, ma'am, but with all due respect for your custom of keeping the Hebrew calendar dates of celebrations, this is the end of the twentieth century, and I have no place in the computer entry for the Hebrew date," this the clerk said definitively.

Malka felt anger rising in her throat. "I'm going in," she said "Please give me the forms. You break your head figuring out the dates without me."

The receptionist, a young woman with wire-rimmed glasses, turned to Yitzhak's identity papers, copied down more than seemed to be there, and returned them with three types of forms. "The first's for the ER; the second is about your obligation to cover the costs of the hospital stay."

She smiled mechanically. "And may the gentleman get well."

Malka took the papers without saying a thing, and without a glance at them. The nurse who measured his blood pressure seemed very efficient, like one of those people who don't waste a minute on purposeless actions. Her hair was cut very short, framing her skull, and she had the face of an eager girl, and a figure so thin that she seemed fragile. She moved quickly. Her Hebrew was fluent, it seemed to come from some other place, and her speech was pleasant. "It's my job to take your vital signs, and assess needs and urgency." Yitzhak opened his eyes, and his face shone as he nodded to Malka. "See, from now on everything will be O.K."

"Thirty six point seven," she declared after barely having touched him with the thermometer.

"What's your name, young lady?" Yitzhak asked.

He looked alternately at Malka and at the nurse, and a touch of pride lit the corners of his eyes.

The nurse giggled, and the brightness of her teeth, as orderly as her actions, won Herzl's heart. Her greenish-gray eyes settled on him.

It was clear to Yitzhak that she had chosen his son as the one who would receive the answer to his question. He looked at Malka and saw her beaming with pride as she looked at her son.

"Here, it says it right here, for all to see, Hagit Lipschitz." She pointed at the nametag stuck on her jacket pocket, a pocket out of which four pens in different colors peeked.

Herzl noticed that she had small breasts. Hagit became suddenly serious. "Both the blood pressure and the pulse are within normal range."

She went out and returned with a medical instrument in a coverless plastic box. Electric wires dangled from it and a piece of tape was stuck on its front. It said, "Please return to the resuscitation unit." Yitzhak's blood froze at the sight of it, and he shut his eyes in order to flee.

Malka sensed his humiliation. "We need help quickly, Hagit. The situation is not good."

Again the nurse looked at Malka's son, and she resolved to overcome her rising irritation.

"First I'll take some blood for tests so you won't have to wait for results later."

Herzl received Hagit's message and used his eyes to send it to his mother.

The nurse wrote with a thick pen on a series of forms bound together with a clip, all attached to a plastic clipboard, alternately leafing through the forms and writing on them. Now she put the clipboard aside and placed jaws of blue plastic on Yitzhak's wrists and ankles, right and left. These were connected to electric wires that first crawled on the sheets and then crowded into the guts of the machine.

A needle trembled over a roll of paper, which had red and white squares inscribed on it.

The murmuring of the strip, freed from the machine, did not deliver good news. Hagit finished.

She undid the connections, tore the strip from the grip of the machine, recorded the patient's name, the date, and the time on it, and then folded it, one half of the strip on the other. She folded it again, until it was easy to clip on. Finally, she clipped it to the binder holding all of the papers.

"There's no emergency," she announced. "You'll have to wait in the area over there until a doctor is free to see you. I have to go get a bed ready. We have an intensive care ambulance bringing a patient in."

She made this last statement quite definitively, leaving no room for further discussion.

The wait seemed eternal.

Yitzhak had curled up in his wheelchair and was leaning forward. Herzl held him up faithfully.

Ever since he had closed his eyes at his recent humiliation, he refused to open them again. From time to time Malka stood in front of him and examined his face.

Herzl realized that this wasn't the best time to try and talk to his mother in any case; he had never been able to carry on a light conversation with her.

After about another fifteen minutes of waiting Malka saw that Yitzhak was sleeping. His tongue was hanging out, and spittle was dribbling from the corners of his mouth.

"I told him he should eat his meals on time ... all those snacks he took while sitting in front of the TV," Malka sighed with eyes cast down. "Just look where all of this has brought us."

And pointing her chin toward Yitzhak, "What didn't I give him? What? The freshest, every day from the supermarket, only so he would eat, only so he wouldn't complain. Vitamins, didn't I buy for him? Of course I did, and non-generic. Anything so he would eat. Didn't I buy everything for him? You bet I did." She coughed and cleared her throat. "And you," she looked up at Herzl, "you didn't know anything. What did you know about it?" Malka raised her eyes and looked at her son. "And your Aviva ... even if she would have known," she hesitated, "it's better that you don't know. As far as she is concerned, I'm better off in the grave."

"Mama, how many times have I asked you to leave Aviva out of this?" He looked away from her. "What does she have to do with all of this stupidity? Leave her out of it!" Herzl scratched his disappearing hair. "If only you would have listened to me ... I would have taken him out of the house from time to time ... so that you wouldn't have turned him into this nothing." Herzl was alarmed at what he had said, and avoided his mother's glance. "Even to go out to the synagogue and volunteer, even that he didn't do." She didn't answer him, and he went on. "When Dad worked in the carpentry shop, he was faster than that Oren, the idiot. If he wasn't Dinah's son, he would have been out long ago." He was almost furious. A touch of spittle glistened in the corner of his mouth.

"Shame on you!" She grabbed Herzl's arm and held on so strongly that Yitzhak, who had fallen asleep, leaned against her and shook. "Dinah changed your diapers when I was sick after you were born."

"Business is business!" he said, and then was quiet.

"Maybe we should get some coffee; there's a machine outside." She hoped he would refuse.

"When a man stays at home you can begin to count the days he has left," Herzl announced. "Look at what happened to Amos Levanon." He looked at her, and she let him know that she knew whom he was talking about. "He left the army at the rank of lieutenant colonel. He was all of forty-three years old, and had a degree in political science. Look what happened to him after six months at home. His wife prays that he will leave the house. He's depressed from morning to night. All day long he's in bed."

"Why are you surprised that his wife has to pray? Isn't she a friend of your wife's?" She said this with a winner's smile on her face.

In the internal medicine ward Yitzhak was lucky to get a bed near the window. "Please, give me a place that's as far as possible from the bathroom," he was saying to the nurse, who had a heavy Russian accent. "I can't stand the smell." The bed was comfortable; the blanket soft. He spent the first hour of his hospital stay sleeping. Malka, sitting, watched over him. Herzl went out to do some errands. He returned after dark. He had showered and put on a white shirt. Aviva was with him. Nurses and doctors came in and out, asked questions, poked and prodded, and wrote things down. In the afternoon Yitzhak said that he had to pee. The nurse behind the nurse's stand signaled Malka with her head. "It's the third room on your left, the chamber pot room. There's no problem, you can just take one by yourself." Malka hesitated a moment, looked to the right and left at complete strangers who were pacing the hallway, and escaped from the ward. On the stairway she put her face in her hands and trembled but didn't make a sound, all alone in the world. She pressed her fingers into her forehead until they hurt and didn't stop until it rang, sharp up her ears. It was a public phone she had been leaning against during all that eternity on the landing, and she hadn't realized it. Malka picked up the phone, as if the call was for her. "Can I please speak to Rachel Revivo in room one hundred and six?" She returned to the ward and found the door locked. A sign hung on the outside, "No visitors allowed during doctors' rounds."

The following day Yitzhak was more relaxed. He was familiar with the hospital routine. "All the nurses here," he complained, "have no legs. As if they are made from the waist up. Everyone is behind a cart, all day long they push those carts, carts made out of plastic and stainless steel, what poor welding work. And the wheels make so much noise, as they wheel them through the corridors. And there is so much on them. Sheets, towels, blue pajamas, also diapers, God forbid, trays of food, medicines, patients' charts, IV bags." Within two days he had become the nurses' favorite patient.

His first meeting with the hospital doctors was strange. The quiet fellow who spoke to him and examined him in the ER on the first day of his stay was so involved in paperwork that Yitzhak couldn't remember his face after he left the examination cubicle. He had felt the small doctor's hammer, the head of which was hard black rubber that struck his knees during the examination. "It's hard to elicit a reflex from you," the young man muttered. "Interesting. You're not a diabetic. Correct?" The doctor went out and returned with a needle from a syringe. "We're going to test your sensitivity to touch. This requires your cooperation." The pricks of the needle in his legs, his abdomen, and his hands were both irritating and exhausting.

"Do you feel this?"

"Yes, I feel it."

"And this?"

"I feel that too."

"And what about now?"

"Everything is fine, doctor. I can feel the pricks clearly." He noticed the drops of blood that had appeared in those spots where the doctor had pricked him too forcefully.

"I'm here because I have no strength, not because of the sensitivity of my skin, if you'll excuse me, please."

"I'm sorry, but this is very important," the man emphasized. The examination took half an hour.

"Thanks a lot. I'll call the doctor ." He finished and Yitzhak pulled his hand away from his examiner's touch.

"And who are you? Aren't you a doctor? Are you a shoemaker?"

"I'm the intern. Dr. Awad will be right here," the young man said dryly. "Don't worry, I'll present the case to him."

Yitzhak saw Awad the following day as he made his rounds in the ward. He spoke discreetly with the nurses and with the doctors, who were only a few years younger than he was. To them he transmitted brief messages, messages whose language concealed more than it revealed.

At nine thirty in the morning of the third day of his hospitalization, twelve hours from the time he had been put on an IV, quiet settled over the ward, and the weekly doctors' rounds began. They came into Yitzhak's room an hour and twenty minutes later, during which time Yitzhak suffered the horrors of the sentenced. During that time he had composed questions and answers, and thought of some witticisms for the doctors and the nurses. But when they came in he was silent, and couldn't find room to get word in edgewise. One of the young doctors even began to suspect that he might be disoriented, and he said as much out loud.

There were eleven participants in this ritual, but only ten remained after one of them left the room, when the black beeper at his waist chirped. A girl with a beautiful forehead and glasses sat on Yitzhak's bed, touching his knees through the sheet. She sat down without asking permission, and didn't give him a glance. Her eyes rested on either the leader of the convoy or on the hardcover notebook in which she recorded what he said. Dr. Goren, about fifty years old, his temples graying, was tall and stooped over a bit. He was serious and severe, and was the center of the group's attention. All conversation was directed to him, and every word elicited his response with a shake of the head, a raising of the eyebrows, and a twitch of his nose and mouth. He and Dr. Awad addressed each other as equals. All of the others asked or answered questions when they were turned to. Twice the leader didn't conceal his opinion of the views of the junior members of the group. His amused responses signaled to the whole group that they should break out in a small burst of laughter. The one who was in this way ridiculed hid his embarrassment with a smile and joined that general laughter.

Yitzhak understood that they weren't talking about him, it was weakness that they were talking about. Weakness of long duration, of short duration, acute, mild, intermittent. The patient who "belonged" to this weakness wasn't Yitzhak, around whose bed they were gathered. Dr. Awad even told of a case of weakness in a woman in labor.

The female student who sat on his bed put her hand on Yitzhak's abdomen and asked, "Can we rule out with certainty that this isn't hypocalcemia in a patient with a malignancy that has spread to the bones from the prostate?"

The participants exchanged glances and nodded at each other.

Yitzhak shut his eyes and saw his life pass in front of him–from the day of his bar mitzvah until his funeral–when he was lowered in a shroud to his grave, while the family stood shoulder to shoulder above him with weeping eyes. "It's all because of the prostate," he whispered.

"Let's check," said Awad authoritatively.

"The calcium results still haven't come back," said Dr. Simon, the chubby one of the group.

"His reflexes don't rule it out."

Awad continued. He pulled out a doctor's hammer from his coat and struck Yitzhak on the knees and heels, first left, then right, and on the right arm. Yitzhak could feel that this doctor's hand was gentler and better trained than that of the fellow who had tested him in the emergency room. "Yes, that's true; the reflexes are weak."

"Has anyone done a rectal exam by finger?" he asked. He waited a minute for an answer and then went on, "Cancer of the prostate can be detected with a high degree of both sensitivity and specificity with a rectal examination." Dr. Goren chastised his charges, "The examination of the patient is not complete."

He waited and listened to the silence of their apology, and continued. "If we can feel a nodule in the gland, the index of suspicion rises considerably, and a needle biopsy for microscopy will be indicated."

Yitzhak's bed partner scribbled furiously, her hand movements as she wrote transmitted to his thigh. They said, "Cancer, cancer of the prostate."

Yitzhak echoed her writing, "Cancer, cancer of the prostate."

"Lift your leg please," said Dr. Simon as he prodded Yitzhak's toe. The female student got up and turned around so that she could see what was going on.

Yitzhak lifted his leg without any problem. It was much easier than on the first day.

During the past two days he had asked to get out of bed in order to go to the bathroom, but was warned against it. "You could fall and break your hip or your head," said the Ethiopian nurse, who smiled with bright white teeth and spoke without a foreign accent. This morning, when the urine bottle spilled on him in bed, he sat up, got out of bed, and stood up. Dizzy, he remained on his feet and didn't give up until the feeling of fright that accompanied this strange instability faded away. The order for frequent drinking was obeyed with confidence, and the cup of tea gradually balanced itself in his fingers.

"There is no damage to the peripheral nerves. " The chief read this from the chart. "Myositis has been ruled out - the enzymes are within normal limits. By tomorrow make sure this patient gets an electromyography." He finished reading, his eyes expressing deep disappointment. "Whose chart is this?" he asked, slowly surveying his audience. "Mine," said Yitzhak weakly, and the group broke out into laughter.

Goren turned on his heels and walked out, and the whole delegation left the room.

"The little old man is a bit confused, isn't he?" Yitzhak managed to hear his young bed partner say to the head nurse, as she helped her push the cart loaded with charts.

Three days after the biopsy was performed under general anesthesia, and two days after he emerged from the fog of it, he found himself still in bed, and subject to the same routine and the same food–yogurt, cheese, tomato, soft-boiled egg, and unsalted porridge–that makes you nauseous. After dinner he got out of bed and stepped barefoot into the corridor. He went out and stood leaning against the wall. Valerie the nurse, about whom he had learned that she had been exposed to radiation in her home country, Ukraine, and who had told him that her sister died two years after the Chernobyl disaster, sat at the nurses' station and wrote. Yitzhak passed by her using the wall for support, and said, "Good evening." She noticed him for a split second, muttered "Good evening," and returned to her writing. Yitzhak continued walking and almost reached the end of the corridor. The journey was difficult for him, and he needed a chair.

Suddenly he remembered his visit to the States, to Jonathan. The elevator broke down, and he, Jonathan, Malka, and Heather, Jonathan's wife, walked up the twenty-eight flights. Malka went up, cursing all the way, and got there first with Jonathan. For a full hour he sat, totally worn out, with Heather on the stairs. They had reached the seventeenth floor, he remembered that distinctly, and

Heather told him about her early childhood in a Christian town in Ohio, and how they later moved to Oklahoma, where she grew up. Yitzhak chuckled at the errors in her Hebrew. "You have them weak feet," she said, as she slapped his knees. Her parents never made their peace with her conversion to Judaism. After that rest on the stairs, he returned to calling her Heather, as she requested, and he didn't permit Malka to call her "Ruth."

Now he looked for Heather, in vain, in the corridor, and was pained that he couldn't find her. He sat in front of the TV at the patient lounge until he fell asleep. Next to him sat a young man with his arm in a cast. He sat there and smoked.

"You have no sense of responsibility."

Malka was shaking him.

"Where have you been? We're all going crazy looking for you." She hugged him, leaning against him with the fullness of her breasts, rubbing against him as she knew he loved. The uniformed guard, who had accompanied Malka until the "lost object" was found, left them alone and was swallowed up in the light of the corridor.

"How did you get here, Yitzhak? How? How?" She hugged him. He put his hands on her hips and returned the hug. "My Malka, now that we haven't done it for a while ... you know ... now it is paying attention ... you know, what's his name, down there, it moves now." He hugged her with such a force that his chair lifted up, the front legs elevated between them.

"You know, they went to look for you in the courtyard, they thought you jumped because of that prostate." Malka smiled. "They saw how sad you were."

She stroked his cheek with her palm. "You poor thing. Listen, everything came out O.K. it's not malignant."

She laughed, "Do you understand? It's nothing."

# CHAPTER 3:

# Meir

*T*hey wheeled Meir into the room while Yitzhak was occupied with a brownish-grey bird that had settled on the marble ledge of the window. Yitzhak heard a hospital aide ask the nurse in the hallway, "I'm putting him in seven, is that what you're saying?" And exactly at that minute he thought the bird had noticed him. He puckered his lips in the bird's direction, as if for a silent whistle, trying to attract the attention of this flighty being, which jutted its beak toward him. "The bird has the eyes of an idiot." He was happy with his discovery and chuckled at the bird, "There are enough professors in this hospital, so this bird can at least even out the average intelligence." He was surprised at himself, at the foolishness of his observations, and wondered whether hospitalization was making him stupid, or whether homesickness was diminishing his sense of logic. He decided to continue observing the bird, but no longer attribute give it human characteristics. But even though he put the plan into action immediately, and the bird turned into a pile of feathers, he was still anxious about his his sanity. When Malka sat down next to him he was a person, and when she left him alone he found a spider in the corner, or a rusted dent in the night table, or even a crumb of bread left over from breakfast on his bed to meditate upon, connect to for companionship, guess their intentions, see absurdity or happiness in the emotions that they failed to hide, but most of all–to worry about them and their predicaments.

The narrow space between the beds and the opposite wall presented a problem to the aides who pulled the beds; they developed wonderful techniques for angling in the mattress-laden iron carriages. When his new neighbor's bed was pushed toward him, Yitzhak didn't see the patient; his head was hidden by the wooden front guard. A rounded shoulder pushed itself behind the person directing the stretcher. "If only God will give me strength for this." It was the wife, it seems, of the new patient; she stood next to him and filled the room with her sorrow. The white scarf she wore on her head in an easy fashion did not fit with the loose flesh of her upper arms, which jiggled to the rhythm of her wailing. She cleared her throat and announced, "We are the Kaminskis" and to Yitzhak, "And what, sir, is your name?"

Even though her eyes were slit and narrow, a greenish-grey of autumn forests budded in him and aroused a distant boyhood feeling that had dulled. The skin on his cheekbones stretched tightly. "I'm Yitzhak, getting out today, at most tomorrow," he said. "Only health, that's the most important thing." She moved herself between the beds of the men. "Do you have a family?" she asked.

Yitzhak straightened his hair. "Yes, yes, of course .

"And a wife?" Her head indicated the area outside near the entrance, but her eyes probed him with their greyness, checking him out cautiously.

"Yes, yes, I have a wife, an three children, a daughter and a son, and another son in America."

He returned to the window, looked around, searched right and left, but the bird wasn't there.

"And what is the gentleman's name?" Yitzhak turned down the institutional sheet from his chest and straightened it out at his hips. "He's very pale, the gentleman, what's his name?"

"Meir Kaminski. We have been in the country sixty-one years come December." Her eyes widened.

"The children were born here," she said. Her teeth revealed themselves in a smile that managed to hide dentures with a slight trembling of pursed lips, with the rubbing of plastic gums.

Kaminski wasn't there with them. He floated above them and beyond, in a journey of lust for air, a journey reserved only for those choking, his eyes closed and a film of cold sweat spreading across the skin of his face and neck, shining like lacquer on a table–lacquer applied to a surface by a practiced hand. The oxygen mask on his nostrils and mouth thickened the lung mist on its transparent greenish side, and with every inhalation the shape of the misty cloud blurred; but it took shape with exhalation, beating with signs of life, in and out. A long rubber tube, dark green, designed to match the shade of the mask with a degree of effort out of place in matters of life on the edge, was well tightened, making sure that Kaminski's spirit didn't mix into Yitzhak's sphere. The tube imprinted a pressure line on what remained of the fat of the skin of his cheeks, tanned from the sun of many years in the land. The ends of the tube, which had no role in encircling the ears, or in embracing the back of the neck, hung for Meir on both sides of his shaved sideburns, the tubes at their edges swinging with the rhythm of his head, moved by the air inflating his lungs.

"Svetlana, Svetlana," called the nurse in training; she was tying a rectangular yellow wooden sign with the letter "S" on it to the guardrail of the bed. "Can you you come here for a minute?" She sounded impatient, and again, "Wow! Svetlana, this new one doesn't look so good to me." She turned to Mrs. Kaminski and pointed with her finger to the door. "Wait outside please, ma'am," and as she said this, pulled the curtain that separated Meir and Yitzhak. "Thank you, and don't close the door. Leave it open, please."

Yitzhak heard the oxygen flow increase, spluttering out into its surroundings, and remembered Malka's thirty-fifth birthday–"twice chai (18) years minus one." He bought her a soda maker in a cardboard carton, its top red, its body silver. And when he created the first container of soda for Malka, how she called out for little Herzl toome and see: "Neshama (soul), come here quickly, this father of yours is like an engineer." Until Herzl got married she called him "Neshama, my neshama." She didn't like the name that Yitzhak had proclaimed in the synagogue, but once Guy was born she stopped "neshama" completely, and maybe even before that, while Aviva was getting rounder in the belly and her hips were widening.

And he closed the container tightly, and turned it over to check that it wasn't leaking, and loaded the "secret of soda" cartridge–small, brown, and cold to the touch–turning, screwing the storage container into the head, and then the secret force burst into the water to make it fizzy. And that recognizable whistling sound before Shabbat, a ritual that was done in the blink of an eye–when thousands of bubbles, created to tickle the throat, were pushed to their drowning fate–became part of the expert's routine of Yitzhak's Fridays. For that reason he assumed that the nurse-in-training turned the oxygen value too high, over the amount she wanted, and only then turned it down. And he also noticed a bubble in the water container for humidifying the oxygen; it was set up on the wall, between the two beds. And after that, quiet. He wondered what was beyond the curtain–now it was quiet–and then he heard the blood-pressure monitor with the air going in and out of the thin tubes of the pump, and after that the friction of separation from the clinging surface of the arm-cuff.

And after that the rhythmic slap of an open palm on the flesh of a cheek, "Do you hear me, Meir?" And again the drumming on skin, echoing bluntly, "Open your eyes, Mr. Meir, open your eyes!"

"Mmmmmmmmm." Meir moved quietly. "Hmmmmmmmm." The moistness of his cough rattled in his voice. The drawn curtain swallowed up Nurse Svetlana, silent as if she were bare foot in her arrival. "What's the blood pressure?" The "L" of her heavy Russian accent was confident and calming. "One hundred and five over sixty, and the pulse is fast and regular, about one hundred and ten!" This from the nurse-in-training with the self-confidence of the very intelligent, and then she hesitated. "Look, but the patient is really in distress, and he's completely wet, just look at this."

"You still have two rooms to do on your side," the one in charge yelled at her. "The chamber pot room is a mess, and then this ..." Yitzhak didn't know what she was referring to. "So listen closely, without any resuscitations and without plans of action on your own authority, please," and she explained more calmly: "Look at his admission notes and see first." She moved away and was heard reading from the hallway, "He was in the ER with pulmonary edema, and then got out, and now he's under morphine, you won't wake him even with a hammer." The younger one pulled back the curtain two-thirds of the way and Meir's dangling hand appeared before Yitzhak's eyes. A bag of urine, and full to bursting, was attached to a pole; a tube escaped from it until it was swallowed up in the bedclothes on its way into Meir. Yitzhak felt thirsty and put out his hand to the clear plastic cup on his night table. The water cooled him, but there was only enough for one lonely sip. For a moment he was sorry that there was only a little water, for if Meir woke up and wanted to drink and there wasn't anyone but himself to help him, he would find his cup dry. Suddenly he was happy that he heard Meir whispering weakly from the other side of the curtain, but he didn't manage to understand what he wanted, or in what language he was muttering–even more so because the voice was muffled in the space of the mask on his nose.

"Mr. Meir, is it possible for me to help you with something?" Yitzhak wondered aloud, and hoped Meir would ask for something that could be accomplished at once, without delay and also without great effort, because he himself wasn't sure of his own powers.

Meir moved his legs under the blanket, right to left and left to right, little movements that had no direction or purpose, and again the right–with small movements here and there–all this while bending a bit, and alternately, his knees, and then straightening them. And again words escaped, mixed with oxygen, louder now, and Yitzhak thought he heard "Why," and again, "Why!"

But the last word wasn't a question, but by way of an answer, taking an explicit stand.

Dusk crept in through the window. This was the time when the doctors came in for their last visit before the change of shift, before turning over responsibility to the night staffer, who would be shut up in his loneliness. Yitzhak knew that at night they made important decisions: who will get discharged and who will remain, who will get X-rays and who ultrasound, who's in for antibiotics through the vein and who for pills to make them urinate, who'll be tied up and who gets pills for relaxation and sleep, who for the urinary catheter and who for the plastic bottle. This time the doctors approached Meir first. The severity of his heavy breathing eased a bit, and Yitzhak's attention turned during the last hour to an old woman from the adjoining room, who called in a thin, high voice, without a stop and with a constant rhythm, "Yamma ... yamma ... yamma ... yamma," and the screen of the doors slamming and opening, emphasizing–muffled and echoing according to a predetermined plan–the constant wailing.

"The new one moves over to the window, so it will be easier with the oxygen"–this stated by an anonymous, mustached person among Yitzhak's visitors–"and this," he said, pointing directly at a point between his eyes, "goes to the big room in an extra bed, and if the chemistry is O.K.

he's discharged tomorrow morning." He pulled a pen out of his lab coat pocket and whispered, "I swear, this patient is here a week, and there's still no answer on his urine results." He wrote down a few words in a notebook whose corners were dog-eared, and added, "People eating for free ... I'm telling you, there are freeloaders here."

Yitzhak was crushed. Why was the doctor so quick to separate them? Now he had a friend and a companion, a fellow soul to share his joys with, and despite the fact that they hadn't spoken, and hadn't even looked in each other's eyes, Yitzhak had already thought of what words they'd exchange when Meir returned to life, and he also organized the sentences he would say, according to their importance to Meir, so that if he got tired of them, and had no strength to listen, he would hear the most important part first, and only the unimportant sentences would be lost between them, and not only that, but he also worried about Meir in his tough time, and he felt better when Svetlana, the nurse-in-charge, came in to check and said, "Now it's O.K." And when she added, "Galit, come for Kaminski; he's lying in feces," Yitzhak didn't get upset, for it was a matter between friends, and how could they separate them, for then each would lie sadly by himself among strangers and sick people.

When the doctors left the room, Yitzhak heard the footsteps of his Malka, "That's how it is when there's nothing to be done," and after her the muttering of Mrs. Kaminski, "If only God in heaven will give us strength."

CHAPTER 4:

# Devorah

"There's a doctor's visit going on, the door is closed."
Devorah leaned against the door, protecting Meir's doctors with her body, so that they wouldn't suffer any disturbance while they were attending to her husband. Not that she blocked the whole entrance, but if someone wanted to open the door even a little–if only to put an eye to the door and glance at the hallway on the left and the four parallel beds on the right–they had to ask her to shift her weight to her left side.

"Move please, madam," Malka hurried, and without waiting for an answer she stuck out her hand and placed it between Devorah and the door handle. She pushed the door open and burst in, her breasts jutting forward.

Deliberately she ignored the group standing around a red-faced young man in the bed near the bathroom, and she ignored the bathroom itself, in which she saw a pair of bony knees in a sharply skeletal pelvis seated on the toilet. On its ankles blue hospital pants were curled up.

They didn't stop her as she walked over to the window, to Yitzhak's sick bed. He lit up with a smile when he saw her. "They may be releasing me," he said heroically. Not a muscle moved in Malka's face. "Look, I brought you some of the apple compote you love so much." She put her basket on his feet, which were covered with his blanket. Diving into the depths of the basket she fished out, as if by magic, a jar once filled with peach jam—the kind of jam it had been very difficult to open. Now it was filled with pieces of apple cooked until they fell apart. They were brownish-yellow and floated in pinkish water.

"It's still cold from the refrigerator." She put the jar down on the night-table and picked up from its flat surface a similar, though empty, jar, which had a wide neck. In it was one pit of the fruit, sprawled on its belly. She opened the empty jar with a gesture that seemed grander than necessary and dumped the pit into one of two flimsy cups, cups which observed jealously the glassiness of their neighbors. Malka took the glass with the pit in it and shoved it into the other glass, pushing both of them to the white corner, close to Meir and away from Yitzhak.

"Tell me, did Herzl come to see you today?" She stared at him until he shrugged his shoulder in a silent reply. "And who is the new one?" She pointed cautiously to Meir, who was breathing heavily. "A very fine fellow," Yitzhak smiled.

"They have been in the city for many years." He pushed the blanket off him, sitting up and almost upsetting the basket. Malka put out one hand to stabilize the basket and with the other helped Yitzhak by supporting his arm. "Maybe he has a contagious disease? It's better to keep your distance until we know for sure." She said this with certitude.

"Ma'am, this is a doctor's visit. Go outside and close the door." A nurse wearing glasses appeared out of nowhere. She was carrying a blue chart under her arm. "I'm leaving my basket on his bed." Malka had stated the condition under which she would leave the room. She bent over, kissed his forehead and lingered a moment to make her departure sweeter. "Did you see her face? How did they decide to let her work here?" Head to head, they both chuckled.

The woman who had stood guard at the door was now seated on a white plastic chair pushed up against the opposite wall. Her hands were on her knees, parallel to each other, and her head was bent forward in contemplation. Her legs were held straight. They were long, with thin ankles, and didn't seem to match the rest of her figure. She wore white shoes with low heels; a wide brown band ran across the width of each shoe.

"You're the wife of my husband's neighbor, right?" Malka stopped in front of her, touching her shoulder with her finger. The woman sitting down looked at the woman who addressed her. "And you must be Yitzhak's wife. He's very, very nice." She looked straight ahead, straight through

Malka's middle. "We are Kaminsky, Meir my husband is sick; oy so sick, and I am Devorah."

"How long has he been sick?" And all the while she left the finger on her shoulder. She put it there to establish contact with her, and now she added another two fingers, so that there were three altogether, stretched out to their full extent in consolation and sympathy.

"Health and luck!" remarked Devorah distractedly. Her attention was caught by the doctor walking by. There was a latex glove on his bloody hand, and he was carrying a porcelain basin. "Only health and luck!"

"And what is your Meir suffering from, and why is he here?" Malka persisted. "Is it something new? Or something he already had?" It took a while for the answer to come: "We've been sick for three and a half years." But Malka didn't relent. "And why here?" Now she placed her whole palm on Devorah, and Devorah responded with the other hand, reaching gently to her own shoulder and touching the comforting hand on which she placed her own, and they stayed like this for a few minutes, the world standing still, and that way everything seemed easier.

"Yes, we've been sick for a long time, my Meir, for years we've been in this hallway, and in others. The nurses here all know us, we're like family. And he also had surgery." She sighed. "Every day, a surprise, day and night, and suddenly he can't get enough air, and he has no strength, and then nothing, and then as if there is no day or night."

She paused, sat up straight in the chair and put her hands back on her straightened knees. "But now, thank God, things are better, things look different."

She changed her mind and returned her hand to where Malka's was, on her shoulder, but Malka was surprised by the action and moved back a bit. "To lose hope is forbidden, for us it's a matter of as long as there is hope in the heart," Malka said, and as she said this she pulled herself away from Devorah's fingers, and her shoulder now consoling itself in its solitude, arms folded over her heart in the oath of an ancient order, soon weakened and her hand fell to her knees, but this time it didn't remain there, but continued to roll on down, and fell to her side, and went on from there, as if devoid of all will, and it kept falling until it fell below the level of the white plastic chair. For a moment Malka lowered her eyelashes as if lost in thought, and then she lit up anew: "You know Devorah earlier I saw your husband open his eyes and look over at my husband?" A long silence ensued. "Yamma, yamma ..." filled the space. "Listen to her crying for her mother. She must be ninety!" Malka was enraptured by the wailing; she showed noticeable joy. "Who knows, she might be a hundred."

The doctors left the door open on their way out. So did the fellow sitting on the toilet, folded over into himself, bent, threatening to break apart. Malka lurched, as if to burst into the room and leave the warmth of the conversation behind, but Devorah, realizing that soon it would be too late to stop her, put out her hand and held onto her friend's hair at the nape of the neck. She didn't mean to hurt her, and was surprised by her own move. All she wanted was to stop her and get an answer to this question: "How do you know that she is calling for her mother?" She noticed that as she spoke her voice changed to a high screech. Malka stopped, turned as if on her axis, and faced Devorah with a serious smile. "What do you mean, how do I know? Everyone, and I mean everyone, calls for their own mother. Who should she call for? Your mother? The minister of defense? The secretary-general of the UN?" With a crooked finger she tapped her forehead. "She called for her mother." And then she recalled: "You know, when I gave birth to my first child, it was only for my mother that I called."

Malka's return instilled in Devorah an uncertain feeling of happiness. "My mother loves Meirke so much! You know, when he walks into a room, everyone stops to hear what he's going to say." She nodded her head and continued: "First of all he's so handsome, like the sun, and the children, may they all be healthy, got from him the faces of angels." She ran her index finger across her cheeks, first across one then across the other. "And they also got their intelligence from him." She brought her delicate eyebrows toward the base of her nose. "On Friday, when he says the blessing over the wine, I look at him and at the children and I think, what luck these children have, such a father, warm, full of light, confident ... like the sun." With her hands she made a large circle in the air; it was as wide as her arms could spread. The wattles on her arms jiggled with her happiness. "And even when I had to hold the bottle over his penis and wash him in bed–you know how men are after their attacks?" Malka nodded in assent–as if she did know, though Yitzhak had never been ill before. "And even when he started to do his number two in diapers, even then, he kept his sunny face." Malka didn't hide that she had stopped listening. She shifted her weight from one leg to the other. "And this was my great fortune, me of the whole family–thank God. Even my mother didn't have–I mean before Hitler, may his name be blotted out–even my mother didn't have such happiness."

They were soon back in their husbands' space, each attending to their own. First Devorah, who straightened the sheet on Meir's toes, uncoiled the oxygen tubing so it wouldn't curl up unnecessarily on his chest, and then ran her hand through his grey hair, some of which had turned black. Malka picked up her bag, which had spilled over on its side, and placed it safely on the corner of the bed. In it she discovered a longish document in green type. "I'm going to the bank to pay the municipal taxes, by foot I'm going. Your son doesn't have time to take me." She said this accusingly, with a blank expression. "It's a three hundred shekel payment." Devorah listened and conveyed this to Meir. He opened his eyes to look at her without blinking. "Do you understand? She goes herself to pay. I don't even know where the bank is. You take care of everything for me, don't you? And I'm happy that everything at home is all right. That's the way it is, isn't it?"

"How can you say that you're so happy, and that he takes care of everything, and that he goes here and there? You just told me that he's been in diapers for two years." Malka was standing with her back to Yitzhak, her voice strong. "So how is that possible? Are you willing to explain?"

Meir put out his hand toward Malka, now alien and angry, as if signaling her to stop. He kept doing this until he calmed his wife down, and then she recovered and hurried to explain. "Do you see what I'm talking about?" She pointed at her husband. "Do you see how he handled things right now? Exactly like he did all along."

"No, I'm sorry, I don't see what you mean at all." Malka put her hands out to her sides and then folded her arms. "Devorah, come outside for a second, there's something you need to know."

"What do you mean?" Her eyes expressed intense curiosity. She was taken by the hand, her body following without will, her white shoes toddling along as if by themselves, until they were outside again, Malka in the lead, her breasts jutting forward, and Devorah stepping lightly, pulled along without resistance. From the women's bathroom, next to their husband's room, which had the number eight, in metal, nailed to the door, a boy and girl emerged, their groins engorged. They walked clinging to each other, side to side, shoulder to shoulder, waist to waist. The girl's head was turned to the side, her lips nursing at his neck, and he–still almost a child–had his long fingers under her armpit on the opposite side, penetrating it from behind and pushing into her and trembling, and they kept walking like that completely unto themselves, and behind them was the constant wail of "Yamma ... yamma ..."

"That's the way we are, look." Malka put out her arm until Devorah too stopped and they stood facing each other. "With all respect to your story and your talk of 'Meir, Meir,' that's the way all the stories are." She softened a bit and held on to Devorah by a button of her blouse. "It starts with a great love, or a small one, and if there is any luck it goes on and on, but then the kids are out of luck, because they are right in the middle of it, and if there's no luck, sometimes it happens that it all becomes one big hate–or a lesser one, one that leaves a bitter taste in the mouth, or, simply, it all turns to nothing, like air, puff ... puff ... You just continue doing what you've been doing, like work, like food." For a moment she lowered her voice: "Like nothing ... like air ... puff ... puff." Her eyes softened, and a note of apology crept into her voice. "And then come babies, and children, and more children, and nursing, and changing diapers, and getting up at night, and food, food, all of the time. Shopping and cooking, shopping and cooking, and shopping and laundry and cleaning up, until they get married and move out."

"In my case the eldest girl didn't get married," Devorah cut in. "She's still cooking at my house." "And in my case he found the worst one possible," Malka went on, pushing at her with her words and her body. "And then all of a sudden you're a grandmother, at first with a lot of energy, helping out, and doing, and calming down, and paying money," and then she lowered her voice, confidentially, "and your husband is still a grand rooster, yes, he's on his garbage heap, and still has all of his feathers, and crows all day long, crowing, crowing, and all day cock-a-doodle-doo, until he gets tired." Her shoulders dropped, she closed her eyes, and silence fell between them. For a moment Devorah thought that she saw a smile on her face. "And after this, this man of yours starts to fall to pieces in your hands, and you run with him to the hospital, and back, and then again, and to the health clinic, and medicines, and examinations, and X-rays, and diapers, until they bury him in the ground. And if you gave him a son, a Kaddish, then you're O.K. as a woman, but if not, something is screwed up with you," and she pointed to her belly–"But first you have to drag him around on your back for a couple of years half-dead till you don't even have strength for the grandchildren." Devorah's face scrunched up and darkened. She bit her lower lip with her teeth, but Malka persisted. "And then you're alone, alone, alone, until your own children become grandfather and grandmother, by then you've been a widow for twenty years with sad clothes, until you're thin and dried up, like this"–she modeled this with her hands on her hips–"until in the end you are screaming in bed 'yamma ... yamma...' just like that one over there, and no one will hear you, that's the way it is ... until that Russian nurse comes and shoves the pill in your mouth so you will sleep."

"You are evil, oh you are such an evil woman," Devorah said in revulsion and pushed Malka away from her. "You are bad, and you have a bad life." She turned her face away from her and toward the wall, her back trembling. "I'm different from that, I'm not evil, I'm not like you, and I've been fortunate in this world." Her voice continued to gather strength. "And I have a good life, and a good husband, and children ..." She fell silent, her face toward the wall.

"Listen to me closely," Malka said. "I'm not evil; rather, you're blind. I'm a queen, like my name Malka, not over others, but only over myself," and she turned Devorah around with two strong hands, turned her toward herself, until they were again face to face, and while doing this lost her balance and almost fell to the floor, but she quickly regained her balance. "And you? What are you? You are Devorah (a bee), also a queen, but a queen of the bees, and all day you have to be sweet everywhere, that there be honey, and then your male bee, for all that he was good to you, drops dead."

Devorah collapsed on Malka's neck and whimpered, her cry in short bursts, like a cough. She stood up immediately and each woman looked into the other's eyes, and they stood that way until the hallway filled with droves of bees, droves and droves, black as clouds, and there were thousands of bees in those droves, beating their wings and buzzing around them in a deafening roar.

CHAPTER 5:

# Kaniel

*H*e looked for his father but couldn't find him. Twice he returned to room number seven, that's what the nurse had told him, "right near the window," and in the bed he saw a Jew with a beard, skinny, with wide-open eyes whose whites were prominent and whose blue pupils were watery blue, and whose cheekbones jutted out over the hair of his beard. He got closer, until the old man looked at him with a surprised expression and whispered, "I'm with Dr. Cohen." He hesitated and then continued, "Here in Haifa." while out the window one could see the flat landscape of the interior coastal plain, very far from Haifa. The plain spread out beyond the eucalyptus trees to the horizon; it was broken only by a line of high poles strung with high-tension wires so heavy they hung in bundles.

He turned around, went out from room number seven into the hall, and saw the tall doctor who had readmitted them two weeks ago (he had forgotten how many readmissions they had had). She had a surprised look in her eyes; she recognized him. "He died last night, didn't they tell you?"

"They told me near the window in room number seven. I looked right now. But it was someone else; a religious man from Haifa."

He felt a slight dizziness, a haziness between his temples.

He tried to steady himself. "Maybe it's the other fellow who died?" And he found himself chuckling inappropriately.

She signaled with her hand–"No, no"–wagging a raised finger from side to side.

"Let's go to the nurse and check." She stepped back to allow him to pass in front of her. "The doctor on call during the night told me that Kaminski passed away." Her walk was faster than her speech. "It was inevitable. I thought they had spoken to you."

The nurses' station was empty. The doctor leaned over the papers and sorted through them as she tried to find his father. He saw her lips move, but didn't hear her. She was pretty, her face smooth and wise.

He shook her outstretched hand and heard, "I'm sorry for your loss." He still held on to her confident hand. "You were a supportive family." Now he heard behind him the sounds of a hospital walker, the footsteps small. "At a time like this a supportive family is very important." The clacking sound came closer, its taps accompanied by the squeak of the light metal, its joints loosened. "The social worker was very impressed by your family's cohesiveness."

ON BOTH SIDES OF THE MIDLINE

She looked at him seriously. "You look pale. Maybe you should sit down for a minute." It seemed to him that the hospital walker in back of him was about to run him over. "Give me your hand, Kaminski, you must sit down." She supported his shoulder.

"I'm Kaniel," he corrected her, his mouth dry. He licked his lips to moisten them. "My dad is Kaminski, and my sister too."

"Your dad was Kaminski," the doctor corrected him. "We understand how hard it is, but it's best that you begin to face your loss." Her hand led him to a wheelchair that stood empty in the treatment room. The sound of the walker kept going; it wouldn't stop. He turned around to protect himself and saw an old woman wearing a wig far too large for the size of her head–it was tilted over her left ear–and with a pink housecoat worn over her hospital gown, Adidas sneakers in which she took short steps. The sound of her walker rattled like artillery.

The sounds of the cannon in Tchaikovsky's 1812 Overture came to his ears. His sister would have read his mind: "You have an Ashkenazi head, and the mouth of a Sephardi thug." Once he sat down in the chair he felt like a complete idiot and quickly pushed aside the back support of the wheelchair. His long legs stuck out beyond the feet supports of this chair for the handicapped. "When you want to get up," the doctor pushed him back down into the chair, "first close the brakes, like this." She leaned over and demonstrated, first on the right and then on the left. Her short hair touched his shoulder; she smelled good. "If you get up without the brakes, the chair will roll back; you could fall and break a leg." She straightened up and made sure with her leg that the chair was stable. "O.K.?"

He sensed that the wheelchair's seat was making the seat of his old jeans wet. "Please don't let it be the urine of the person whose chair it was." For a moment he was afraid that the patients marked their chairs, as dogs marked their territory, and that he had to smell the chair first to make sure.

"You have a strange hospital here," he said to the doctor, and to himself.

"The color has returned to your face; you feel better, don't you?" Her victorious smile made the point that she had been correct. He understood then at once that father had died and that there was an urgent need to see what was going on with his mother, who was alone at home, or maybe with Rachel, and how was it that they hadn't let him know? Maybe his cell phone was off; he turned it off every Friday. "You're going to be a great doctor," he said to her with enough confidence to get out of the chair and to make it clear that from here on in he was in control. He got up and felt his backside. His hand felt moisture, be brought it to his nose and sniffed. "It's not urine. It seems that it's water." The doctor smiled. "I was afraid that I sat down in ..."

"It's from the cleaning woman. She's very careful, very thoroughly washes the chairs and beds of the deceased before they go to a new patient." She discovered something, and her face lit up. "Look." She pointed at a wide strip of white tape that was stuck on the back of the chair. "This was his."

"Meir Kaminski" was written in the large script used by new immigrants, some of the lettersthe aleph crooked, the yod after the mem missing. "She must have cleaned it after he died and forgot to take off the tape." She scratched at the corners of the tape and tore it off. A sharp pain went through him, as if tufts of hair from his curly chest hair were being torn out, hair by hair, as he heard the cloth separate from the plastic. It hurt so much that he clutched his chest, and then the pain subsided, and he felt better. She smiled at him. "It was only water, maybe with a little cleaning solution in it, but surely very diluted." She rolled the piece of tape between her palms until it rolled up into a ball and then tossed it into the basket under the nurses' desk. "It won't hurt the skin at all, don't worry." He still had his hands up in front of his chest, protecting himself, his eyes wide open and staring at father's chair.

"Let's see if they have arranged the matter of the death certificate," she said getting right to the point. "Your mother, that's what they told me, was here when he died."

What she had said earlier still echoed in his ears. "A supportive family ... family." He didn't know where his fragile mother got the strength to sit by his father's bed during those last days and nights, snatching bits of sleep as she dozed in the chair at his side. In the afternoons, when Racheli took over, she went home by bus, showered, changed her clothes and, it seemed, slept for a few hours. Racheli was impatient until her mother came back. "Why are you in such a hurry, Rochele?" her mother chastised her when she returned to her post beside the bed. That was just five days ago, when he came to take her to the hospital in his car on his last visit to father. "What are you in such a hurry for? You have no husband to feed, no children's diapers to change, and your piano won't run away anywhere." "So you say that we were a good family, huh?" he asked the doctor. "Definitely," she said forcefully, "But supportive, that's the right expression, not good. Good is another matter, not in the area of our expertise." She turned to him. "Who knows what a good family is?"

He didn't notice that she was rifling through the batch of papers. "I see that they took the death certificate ... it seems that your mother took care of it before she went home."

"Tell me," he said tensely, "when I was here a few days ago, father was very pale and sweaty, and he kept taking off the oxygen mask; it bothered him terribly." All of a sudden he felt angry. He swallowed his spit. "He was very uncomfortable that day. Were all of you at all aware of that?" His voice rose. "Did you try to do something about it?" And then he remembered. "I was there holding his hand."

"Your anger is understandable, Mr. Kaminski," the doctor said. She sounded distant and curt. "You are entitled to express anger or hostility, if you wish, and it's our job to accept that, if it helps you, of course."

"I'm not trying to assign blame," he explained. "It's important to me to know if you did everything possible." He felt that he was being dishonest. "In any case it's too late–for him or for us."

"Look, Mr. Kaminski ..."

"Kaniel," he corrected her.

"Look, Kaniel, we talked with your mother and with your sister. The past few days have been difficult, and we expect the family to transmit information in its own way." It sounded logical. "We are not responsible for what goes on between you. The social worker was also there when we talked, her name is Revivit." She stopped for a moment and furrowed her brow. "You must have met?" she asked, or declared.

"No" he shot back, "I've never heard that name, and we don't need a social worker to explain to us that father is sick. And also ..."

"Excuse me," she cut him off, "I have a lot of work." She hesitated, looked at him, and then glanced down at the sheaf of papers. "He had pulmonary edema/water in the lungs twice in the past few days, and don't forget that he was eighty-one years old."

"Seventy-seven," he corrected her weakly, and he remembered how his father had taught him to swim in the ocean, holding him by both hands and yelling, "Now, kick quickly with your legs," and how his full black hair got wet and was plastered across his forehead. "Look, he still had most of his teeth. Until recently he was strong as an ox. On Passover he would move the furniture around by himself, so that mother could clean near the walls."

"He was very ill, sir. In the echocardiogram of the heart they saw that his heart was as weak as a dish rag," she explained. "The ejection fraction was only twenty-four percent. It's hard to stay alive in that condition."

He was embarrassed: he thought his father had had a disease of the lungs; he had had trouble breathing when he came to the emergency room. "So you're saying it's all from the heart?"

"They call it ejection fraction; it's the index that shows how the heart muscle is functioning."

"I'm sorry for that outburst, doctor. You are ... really, all of you are O.K." He decided that he had to hurry to his mother at home.

He put out his hand and she gave him a powerful handshake. "Thank you, doctor," he said, and turned to leave through the main door of the ward. A cleaning woman in a blue smock was moving a mop with a rag on it back and forth as he passed her. She looked at him, and as he passed he heard her voice. "Excuse me, sir, but are you the son of Kaminski, may he rest in peace?" He couldn't quite identify the very un-Israeli accent. "Excuse me, sir."

"Yes, that's me." He took a single step and leaned against the wall.

She rested her cheek on palms, which were placed on the mop stick. "Your mother is still here from last night; she felt sick when the gentleman died, so they took her to the emergency room." She went back to her work, swinging the mop from right to left. "Maybe you should go there," she almost whispered. "Maybe, so she isn't miserable all on her own."

He didn't walk out quickly. In the area across from the elevators, sitting on the benches set aside for those who were waiting, sat a patient in a hospital gown. In his hand was a newspaper, which he was reading with great interest, his head at an angle. "Looks like the weekend magazine," he thought. He went closer to the elevator door and pressed the lower button of the two. A red arrow, pointing downward, lit up: "From dust you have come and to dust you will return." The patient turned a page of his newspaper and discovered a large photo of the minister of education; it filled the bottom two-thirds of the page. When the elevator door closed he recognized the reader as Yitzhak, his father's neighbor from two days ago, and he felt a surge of emotion that he couldn't identify. The elevator door opened, and he walked out all churned up, his palm to his forehead. He stood for a moment, and realized that in error he had gotten out on a floor in the middle of the building. He turned toward the Emergency Exit sign, pushed the metal door, and found himself in the stairwell, and from there he went down to the first floor.

## CHAPTER 6:

# Malka

A ll during the week, which had started on that day, she recalled the sensation of hot coals hurting the soles of her feet. As that day began she shook like a kettle before it's about to boil. From exactly noon onward, when she checked her watch and saw that they were very late, she walked around and stopped, turned on the spot, faced the window, shot a glance at the courtyard, leaned on the wall of the hallway and then switched to the opposite wall, returned, sat down, and got up again. How well she remembered going up and down the stairwell of the hospital. Twice she went down and twice she went up. First just one story, and then another four steps, and then she returned to where she had started from; but the second time she hurried up all five flights. She didn't return all the way to the ground floor, but to the area above the X-ray department from where you could see the feet of those waiting for the elevators. There she took off her left shoe, leaned to the right on her arm and breast against the railing, and slowly and gently rubbed the sole of her foot with her left hand; first, with a circular motion, rubbing around the hard areas around the heel, and then rubbing from the periphery to the center, then massaging it again, and finally massaging from the sides to the center–and then repeating the whole process three times. And she listened to the burning sensation that popped like a fried egg left so long in the pan that its edges, and the oil around them, turn dark and start to bubble, sending up steam and a sound, and for a moment she felt that she could hear these sounds, and while she was still paying attention to how she felt she checked the padding at the end of her toe, looked and checked it again, and the fire subsided.

During the week that followed, she remembered that when she finished taking care of herself, she was filled with pride that only her own willpower rendered her able to cope with this world. Despite the fact that she was getting stronger, she arrived worn out, as if she hadn't slept all night, though all the time Yitzhak was a patient she found sleep a sweet refuge, and she wondered whether it was because sleep was something that her body demanded from her spirit, or possibly it was the other way around–her spirit was telling her body to sleep well and gather strength for the days to come. And that whole climb back to the internal medicine ward, step after step, was difficult and drawn out; her knees threatened to collapse under her, and she put out her hand to hold on and steady herself, and the very hand that had saved her from the burning sensation in her shoes, her left hand, pulled her upward for two or three flights, and she lifted her eyes to see that there was only one flight of stairs to go, and she had never known such joy, the joy she got from that left hand, and the whole thing made up for a whole life of not putting tefillin on her left hand, the way her father did–and as the other men did, men who said the blessing praising God "who has not made me a woman," for their left hands were closer to their hearts and their God than her left hand. At that moment she stood up straight and with a smile she took out from the left-hand pocket of her purse a tube of hand cream. She held it in her right hand, turned the cap with her left, put it between her teeth and squeezed out an inch from the soft tube, then turned the tube on the cap stuck between her teeth, closed her eyes for a moment, and gave the palm of her left hand the oiling and massage that it had been so in need of for the last hour. She began with the index finger of her right hand, which pushed the oily snake of lotion on to her concave, thirsty palm, until the cream became a crooked star with five horns, two of them–the shorter and closer ones–pointed to the thumb, which was limp with pleasure, and three other horns were squashed, one at the base of the pinky, and two lifting up like twins on the slope of the palm which looked down from its reddened callused height to the sharp slope down to the lines that crossed the width of the palm. And right away, before cold could set in, the fingers of the right hand went to work rubbing it into the deserving skin.

At the stairwell of the last floor her grip on the railing slipped, so she had to use both hands, the oiled one next to the dry one. The bag on her hips pushed against her, and though the vector of her exertion was opposed to the direction she was headed, somehow, with the strength of the bag she reached the entrance.

"You were supposed to check on your husband three hours ago, ma'am, said an Ethiopian Nurse. "He's been sitting in the dining area for an hour and a half, and you're running around."

Yitzhak was taken home by a private ambulance ordered by the assistant head nurse, who made sure to say that "that's with the resident doctor's O.K., the ambulance." She handed Malka a sealed envelope from the hospital. I`m sorry, there's a sick patient coming up from the ER, Yitzhak's bed is now taken, we told you this two days ago." She patted Yitzhak's shoulder as they left her kingdom and went to the waiting area. "And stay healthy for me."

"Many thanks for everything," Yitzhak smiled. "And also to Marina and the doctor if you ..." The aluminum door closed on her sparkling teeth and the elevator descended. The door opened at one of the floors, and in front of them stood a man dressed in blue overalls standing behind a plastic garbage container. He looked at Yitzhak in the wheelchair, looked without saying anything and without moving, until he disappeared behind the door.

"I don't know him," Yitzhak looked at Malka's arms, which were wrapped crosswise around her bag. "Finished with the hospital," he added. "At home I'm alone, with no one's help."

Malka sat next to the driver, who didn't stop telling stories she didn't hear, and she surveyed the two sidewalks of Herzl Street, looking closely so that she missed nothing, even what was behind a parked truck, turning her head back so far that she had to turn her shoulders after it. She felt good in the slow thick traffic, where nothing escaped her attention, not even one pedestrian, not on the shady side, and surely not on the sunny side, even though the shady side was the distant one, on the other side of the talking driver, and she couldn't see as much from his window as from her own. And when Sasson the driver–it turned out that that was his name–unloaded Yitzhak from the bowels of the ambulance, it was clear to Malka, without a shadow of a doubt, that no one on the street escaped her scrutiny, even if they were standing with their back to her and were facing a store window; and when they arrived she scurried to the entrance to the building and hurried up to the locked door.

At the carpentry shop Salim answered; she hung up, pressed the redial button, and again it was the Arab. "Where is Herzl? It's urgent." She found that she was in complete control of her voice.

"Not at work today, Mrs. Malka." She thought about the fact that Salim was always polite and considerate, and that his shirts were always clean. For a split second she wondered if she would marry an Arab. "God protect us," she muttered, and hung up the phone. She dialed 6, knowing that the dialing takes longer when it's direct. She heard Guy's voice. "Dad's not home, do you want Mom?" He called Aviva without waiting for her answer. "Grandma Malka wants Dad." She heard the TV in the background, the sound of house slippers on the floor, and again Guy's sigh. "Mom says Dad's at work."

"Thanks, sweetie, see you soon." She saw Aviva driving and crashing into a truck carrying chickens, and saw a cloud of white feathers falling on her dead face through the shattered window of her car. "It's too bad about the car, it was nice and new." Sunlight from the living room rested on the embroidery picture, as it always did in the afternoon, and she knew that it was three, or almost four.

On the toilet she wondered where she got the willpower not to pee; the urge had been building all day from the time she entered the hospital until right now, her strength fighting the pressure rising from her abdomen. She pressed her thighs together until the urge was conquered. This was the second time today that her body had tried to get the best of her, and she won. On a normal day, when she wasn't being tested, early in the cold morning, when the grey light gives in to the lowered eyelids of the blinds, and the urine pushes her quickly out of the sheets, so that it just doesn't pour out, but today, nothing can get the better of her and she beats it both internally and externally.

"Oy vey," she remembered now that the door was closed, Sasson the ambulance driver must be bringing Yitzhak up the steps. She wiped herself with toilet paper, checked it as she always did, then wiped herself again, and couldn't find the strength to stand up. She bent over and grabbed the sink, pulled and straightened herself out, arranged her clothes, washed her hands and noted that her left was smooth and her right dry. There was no towel, so she went to the bedroom, hesitated and chose a green towel, went back to the bathroom and hung the towel on the plastic hook attached to the tile with a suction cup. "That's all I need now, for him to fall down, that's all that's missing."

On the stairway there wasn't a living soul. She went to the kitchen patio; beyond the hanging laundry she couldn't see anyone. She leaned over far in order to see. "Morons," she said, and again loudly, "idiots, morons," she was almost screaming. She realized that she was in danger of falling over and was taken aback. She checked the marble of the railing, "very stable, old style construction," and patted it approvingly. Mechanically she pulled off the clothespins with the grace of a trained pianist, pulling off a towel from the right, a shirt from the left, a pair of pants from the middle, and again from the left, right, and center, tossing the clothespins with a clang into the cracked porcelain bowl at her feet, all of this with the grace of an artist, not losing a clothespin, and the clean scrubbed clothes piled up on her neck and more piled up above her breasts, the clothes held tight by her neck. "Idiots, that's what they are."

She hugged the laundry with her hand and freed the muscles in her neck. She tossed the laundry down on a couch in the living room, the one with its back to the TV, and pulled out Herzl's white shirt. "We'll iron it for him, so he will look handsome," she told herself. She freed the iron and the ironing board from their crouching place in storage, and plugged it in. "Heat up, you bastard."

She went out to the stairway and returned to the iron in the living room without hesitation. "I'll set it on synthetic, so it doesn't get too hot." She checked the fabric control dial–"Synthetic." And again to the stairway where she checked the short distance between the stairwells, and except for the stroller tied up with a chain, which belonged to the seamstress from the first floor, nothing responded to her.

She grasped the latch of the electrical panel, lifted her head, puckered her lips and for a long time filled her lungs with air–it whistled into the cavities of her nose down, down; she puffed up, and a small spider held on to its web, which shook on the opposite door. Her shoulders rose and spread out to the sides and all at once the whites of her eyes turned red, and two blue veins, widening and engorged, spread out from the sides of her neck to behind her earlobes, and her chest battered against the restraints of its bindings.

"Yitzhaaak!"

The stroller on the first floor shook against the metal railings, and the door of the electrical panel on the second floor opened on its hinges and banged against the wall.

She began to iron the shirt at the collar. From there she turned to the front of the shirt to the row of button loops, to the right and the left, and then she moved to between the buttons. "Not Herzl, this doesn't suit him." She spread out a wide sleeve with surprise. "He knew that Yitzhak was being discharged in the afternoon. And I also told him this morning; he heard every word on the phone." Hurriedly she doused a tear with the iron, and then again another one that fell and stood out on the fabric and wasn't absorbed by its fibers. He said, "Don't worry, Mom, everything will be O.K." The iron hissed with the steam of her tears for a third time, and then again. "Everything's O.K.," he'd said; she hurried to turn over the other sleeve before the tears dried and she laughed to herself: "Everything's O.K." she said to the shirt fabric, "so wide," and her cries were sufficient for the whole shirt, and even enough for a second ironing of the collar.

"Thanks, Avigdor, and you stay healthy–you and the family." Yitzhak said goodbye to his Bulgarian neighbor, but the neighbor stood there stubbornly in the entranceway and kept pressing the hall light switch. "Really, thanks a lot, to here is fine."

"Look at the shirt, as if it's from the store," she went out to them victoriously–"Come on in." She waved them in with her arms stretched out in front of her. From the entrance Yitzhak could see her head–up to her nose, her fingers at the corners of the fabric, from there on it was a blank white screen until her thighs–and then the flowery hem of a skirt.

"I'm sorry, Mr. Avigdor, look, I forgot my left shoe in the restroom. It's dangerous to iron when you are barefoot; there's a danger of electrocution." She carefully hung the shirt on the back of the chair. "Now you can both come in."

Yitzhak made his way into the bedroom, holding on to the walls while taking small steps. "It's the envelope from the hospital, you left it next to the driver," he said, and put it on the dresser. "It's a good thing that I noticed." He made sure that the edges of the envelope were lined up with the edge of the dresser. He lingered a moment to fix it, again making sure that it was lined up.

Now he was standing at the window. "The door was shut." He looked out at the empty space; he had thought that Malka was standing there. He repeated himself: "The door was shut." Without bending over he got one slipper off and then managed to shake the other one off in the same way and then he lined up the slippers with the toes next to each other. When he freed himself from his socks it seemed to him that the skin of the tops of his feet were looking at his face, and that his face was looking at the tops of his feet, and that they had found each other and were both shining as if some half-opaque dandruff powder had settled on them.

"After he saw, Mrs. Malka, that it was locked, the Magen David ambulance brought him to me," Avigdor explained. "Your tea is excellent," he sipped, "excellent, and also delicate, not too sweet." He sipped again, "and the driver wasn't at all angry."

"Here, take some of the biscuits," she took a piece broken off at an angle, "dip it in the tea." Then, after a moment's wait, she returned it to the plate she had placed on the telephone table. They drank standing up. "Really, thanks for taking care of Yitzhak." She gave him a crooked smile, like someone sucking on a strand of meat stuck between their grinding teeth. "I'm sorry, all of this tension in the hospital, no one ..." She drank from a cup about half the size of Avigdor's. She felt for the napkin underneath the tea pot, smoothed its edges and scratched at no real spot with her fingernail. "Just imagine that for two days the laundry has been hanging on the balcony. Who could imagine that such a thing could happen with me?" She smiled apologetically. "Also–I was, if you'll excuse me, in the bathroom, the hospital bathroom just wasn't for me ... you know, the whole day."

He smiled and thought he saw something spark in her. He came close enough for her to see the pores of his shiny forehead. He handed her his cup and she stood facing him with two cups in her hands. She moved her hands away from her hips–until he could see, between her steaming armpits, the wallpaper facing him.

"Tea is good for every occasion," he smiled. "I make myself tea in the morning and in the evening." He stuck out his palms, one facing the other, and trapped the sides of her breasts as if he was measuring the distance between them, looked at what he had done, raised his eyes to her face, and then again to her chest and then wandered and climbed with his index finger until he reached the summit, and made circles against the hard surface of her thick bra–so thick that he couldn't feel her nipples hardening.

"Take, finish, drink," she handed it to him at the level he was groping her. She looked at the shuttered window. "It's hot, it's already two days that it's been hot."

He took it with his left hand, but left his right hand on her. "For the young girls today a T-shirt is enough, and you can lift it up quickly, without any problems." He held the cup in both hands and sipped, kept it near his cheek, waited until he sipped for a long time, coughed and his spit splattered on her arm. She wrinkled up her nose in disgust, and he carried on. "The Christians in Bulgaria, their churches with grand domes, and on these tits they place Jesus' cross, and from the time that they are little they are drinking/nursing their god along with the milk."

"Are you a monster, or a human being?" she asked with no facial expression. "Your Stella, she had a good life, didn't she. How she'd scream at night." She turned to the kitchen and put down the empty cup. "I'll never forget the smell of her cooking."

She poured out two-thirds of a cup of tea into a white mug; on it was written "The sign of Pisces." She sipped only a little, as if she was estimating the heat of the drink, and walked toward the bedroom. Yitzhak sat on the open bedspread and pursed his lips toward her.

"You like it that I bring you stuff to drink, huh?" She caressed his forehead. "O.K., O.K., today I'll pamper you just one more time, that's it." You came back to me a hero, not a child." He took a little sip, and then one more. "It's enough for me, Malka, thanks."

*CHAPTER 7:*

# Salim

"He didn't eat the omelet and drank only half of the yogurt," thought Malka as she moved the tray from the living room to the kitchen. From the slice of bread, on which she spread for him the cream cheese with 5% fat, the cheese advertised as velvet, the cheese that covered all the pores of the bread, from this piece he ate only the center, like a nibbling rat. He left the hard ring of crust, but he didn't tear it; he licked the cheese off it, as if he knew that she would be less irritated if he didn't leave the cheese on what remained of the slice. "Mother has respect for bread"-that's how Yitzhak educated the children. He himself constantly told them, "Work means bread."

Only after Malka cleared away the leftovers of Yitzhak's meal and threw it in a bag, the one used only for scraps of vegetables and fruit-it sat on the counter to the right of the sink, and you weren't allowed to throw plastic milk containers into it-only then did Malka realize that she was angrier than she first thought; Yitzhak was upsetting her usual routine. Quickly, she called Herzl at the carpentry shop. "Everything is on my head to take care of."

The new worker didn't know who she was, and she didn't know who the hell was answering the phone. "I'm new here, ma'am, I'm sorry that I can't help you." She slammed down the phone without thanking him, and without leaving a message. In any case, she didn't reach Herzl and she also didn't learn if Herzl had come in that morning; if he was there or if he was out on errands. Recently these errands seem to take up much of his time, more time than she thought appropriate.

On the bus she discovered–to her intense irritation–that she had forgotten to take her head kerchief, the light one. It was blue and almost transparent. Usually she carried it in her purse, but when she was home she always was careful to free it and air it out. "So what, that idiot Rotenberg has a little dog that she takes out twice a day. At least my kerchief doesn't make a mess!"–this comment she threw out once to Aviva.

The bus stopped to let passengers off in the middle of the street–a motorbike that was delivering pizza was parked at the bus stop. From a distance she saw the gate of the carpentry shop's courtyard; the gate was opened wide enough for a person to pass through, but not wide enough for signs and furniture, which needed more space so that they wouldn't get scratched. "In Yitzhak's days it was open wide," she remembered with sadness; quickening her footsteps she opened both wings of the gate, pushing them until they crashed against the fence, and then she fastened the gate to the latches that Yitzhak had put in for just that purpose.

She passed through the entranceway, her manner stormy. Salim didn't dare say hello to her. He lowered his head to the iron press, placing into it a board longer than he was tall. When he noticed her, he put his face closer to the wood, even though he knew that because of her experience, Malka would see the ridiculousness of leaving so little space between the board and the tip of his nose. She passed through the empty gluing room, and with two sharp steps went up the three iron steps that led to the office. She opened the door. A pencil, orphaned without its memo pad, hung from a piece of string tied to its nail. The blinds were shut carefully. She moved them aside with her finger and saw Salim watching from a shadowy observation point in the far corner of the gluing room. Herzl's desk stood abandoned, yearning for the days when Yitzhak was there. A bunch of receipts of different sizes and random shapes, held together by a white plastic clothespin, lay on the cardboard blotter that Herzl changed whenever it filled up with notes and smiley faces. She noticed that he had changed the blotter a few days earlier; the new one had little on it. One receipt had separated from its friends; on it was the silver Parker pen that Herzl received from Aviva on the day that Yitzhak handed over the office to him. Again she saw the shadow of Salim, who was, uncharacteristically, not doing anything and looking directly at her. A light, checkered purple sweater peeped out at her from the guest chair across from the desk. Under it peeked a small purse made of soft brown leather. "Aviva's it's not," she was sure of it, and a smile of victory spread across her face. The worries of the past week were erased from the corners of her mouth. The sweater was inside-out, and the manufacturer's label hung from the lips of the back collar. On a strap on the front of the purse there was a plastic bracelet, of the type that they put on newborns in the maternity ward so that they don't go to the wrong mothers. She gave birth to Herzl at home; but Jonathan was born in the maternity hospital. He was so fair, she was afraid that he was given to her in error. From the day he went off to distant America these old doubts assaulted her. Today, with these plastic bracelets, they don't make mistakes and switch kids. "He's as stubborn as I am, Jonathan," this was how she consoled herself, "and he has my eyes, too." Now she heard rustling in the worker's locker room. She heard a man's voice and moved closer; as she moved she marked out with her finger a corner of the sea of papers. For a moment she thought that she recognized Herzl's voice, but no, the sound came from the outside. She noticed that he had hung up the photo of the president. The photo showed an old man; he was older in the photo than he was in her mind. With sure steps she walked through the entranceway marked by clear plastic strips. They hung down from the over-hanging beam, their edges worn down at different heights. She shook her head: "He's clean, may he be healthy, but the office is a mess." She shook her head. From across the bathroom corner a weak light was shining. Herzl was there, and some other figure with him. He sat on a black seat that had been torn out of a truck. The seat, without legs, was dumped into the room; it fit perfectly into the space between the lockers where the workers stored their clothes and possessions. His head was thrown back and his eyes closed. "He's not as handsome as Jonathan," she thought, "but he definitely has the nobility of the family face." His forehead was wet and his long legs, with his shoes on them, stuck out from the low seat. His knees, bare down to the calves, peeped out–hairy and firm–over his turned-down overalls, his white underwear on top of them. "Always, even as a child, he changed his underwear every day, sometimes twice a day, and I washed them," she remembered. "He should only be healthy. I never said a word to him about it."

His hands were holding on to the hips of the thin woman, she was naked from the shirt down, and she sat on his pelvis with a confident posture, her two hands on his shoulders and her head held erect. The skin of the thigh facing Malka was remarkably smooth and firm and her shoulders were lovely as she moved. Malka wasn't embarrassed, but stood there watching the two of them, watching with a mother's pride the creature she had produced.

A large balloon with Aviva's face on it burst in the air, and fell to the ground without a sound.

Herzl groaned once, and in it was a mixture of sadness and self-control; she hadn't know that one of her own could produce these sounds. The slight woman moved up and down on him to the muffled sound of her thighs, and for a moment she lost her balance and with her left hand steadied herself against the metal cabinet which was pushed up against the wall, and she bumped into it a few times in her upward and downward motions, until Herzl opened his eyes about halfway and smiled with a happiness she didn't know he was capable of, and then he moved the unknown woman's elbow, and her arm came down on him until he brought her hand back to his shoulder, and then he fell back and closed his eyes. "What silence, like two strangers," and she almost felt sorry for her son.

She turned around and went out, scanning with gravity the area of the carpentry shop from her position at the office door. She closed it carefully, so as not to make a sound, walked down one step of the three steps that led to the gluing and assembly room, and stopped to look in her purse, searching through it for a long time, looking to the right and the left, as if she couldn't find what she was looking for. "No one is going through this door until my Herzl is finished." She stood up straight. In her purse:

store receipts, lipstick, a pen, keys, hospital forms, mixed with Dr. Sovrin's prescriptions. She took out the tube of the Velveta cream and found that the cap was loose. She tightened it well. Then she returned it to her bag, closed the clasp, and placed it like a tray on her raised right leg, which she placed one step higher than its twin.

The gluing and assembly room was empty. She stood at her post for about five minutes, until she heard voices from the office space. No one had come in. She remembered the busy room in Yitzhak's days, when they were gluing pieces together: Boys were carrying the boards in and out; Adele, who was retarded, was cooking the various glues in the corner until they started using ready-made glue, and the labor of the Arabs of Gaza, until the curfews of the Intifada, and until the murder of the secretary of the aluminum company by an Arab worker in Holon, and Aviva decided that there would be no more gluing, they would buy everything already assembled–it was cheaper, and with no headaches. Yitzhak didn't forgive Herzl for doing away with the gluing.

She shook herself awake. "It's important to use the room the way it was once used," she decided, and she walked down into the orphaned space, opened the east window and brightened it. The rays of sunlight lit up the particles of dust that she had raised crossing the room.

"Salim!!" she called out, "Salim, come here! Leave everything, pour out water on the floor–even in the corners; let's clean the place until it shines."

Salim arrived. He was wearing a slightly confused smile of great relief. She noticed that his hair had thinned a bit. She was surprised when he took her hand in his, and covered it with his other hand. "Please tell Yitzhak to get well soon, you know ..." He let go of her hand, "I didn't want to bother you in the hospital. Tell him I'll come visit at home."

"Look, this room isn't used at all. We need to clean it, air it out, and then maybe Herzl will be inspired to make use of it." She tried the light switch and the blind lamp in the metal shade that hung from the wall; it didn't respond.

"And there's no light here," she said angrily.

"I'm opening the windows, Mrs. Malka, like this," Salim said. The iron bolt clanged and crashed, and the heavy shutters turned in their fittings with a rusty sound. "Here, like this. And now the other one." He crossed the width of the room and she noticed that when he leaned against the windowsill a line of grey dust marked his blue overalls. "Just a minute, Salim." She came closer. "Wait a minute." She reached him and brushed off the dust on his clothes. She did it once, and then again, from top to bottom, and again from side to side, until it came off.

"Thanks, Mrs. Malka," he smiled. When you're here the light comes back into the carpentry shop. See, look at it now."

A short cry escaped her lips–"Aah." She stopped it with her hand so as not to let it escape. The moment stretched out and they stood facing each other, his eyes on her, and her eyes searching the walls that were so recently lit up, until she cleared her throat and smoothed her skirt against her thighs. "Really–please come and visit Yitzhak at home, he's all alone with himself. He'll be happy to see you."

"We'll get there, we will, if God wills it." They continued standing too close for the dimensions of the room.

"I'll make you good coffee," she promised, and smiled until she laughed, and as her laughter continued, she bumped her head affectionately against Salim's shoulder and went on her way.

Herzl watched from the door of the office, standing on the third and top step, Malka's back to him. She walked to the left of the wide assembly table and went on without stopping, and Herzl folded his arms across his chest and watched her until she crossed the wood-storage room and went out. Salim too stood where he was, looking at the boss.

"Your mother is a good woman," he said to Herzl with a smile. "Listen, Salim," the boss said after contemplating the Arab's expression, "from tomorrow on you are running the business. I'll be out of the country for about two weeks and you don't know where I am." For a moment his face looked different than ever before. "Is that clear? You don't know anything." For a moment he looked different than he ever had. Salim was taken aback. "Is that clear? You don't know anything." Salim made a gesture that indicated that everything was in the hands of God.

"And something else, make sure that my mother, Mrs. Malka, has everything she needs."

Hagit crossed the room with light steps, paying no attention to the two of them, and then went out, as if she didn't know anyone there.

# CHAPTER 8:

# Nadia

"Very tasty, very," Nadia indicated as she took a piece of cake. It was so thin and flaky that its corners had rounded. She held it near her mouth, three fingers supporting it from the bottom and her thumb supporting it on top, her pinky off to the side, uninvolved, and while she hesitated, the back of her hand toward the onlookers, her mouth half open, lusting after something wonderful, and her eyes looking right and left to see what effect she was having, a tiny piece of cake fell on that part of her skirt draped over her thigh, and continued on its gradual descent to the carpet, where it broke into two pieces, one three times larger than the other, and though the larger piece fell near her black patent leather shoes, which were touching each other, and a large gold buckle, devoid of any fastening function, but placed there for beauty, stuck out in front of them, the piece of cake kept rolling, covering a distance far greater than its size, until it found its rest near the right leg of the chair on which Avigdor sat, silent and withdrawn, with his knees splayed open.

For the past four days Malka had been occupied with Meir Kaminski's death, which had been announced on the mourner's notices tacked up on the main street and on the trunk of the tree near the library. There was one small notice put up by the friends of the deceased from the local Bnai Brith society. It described him as "a man of many talents," and another notice, larger and more detailed, saying "the crown of our glory has fallen," with the exact time of the funeral, and also, "we are sitting Shiva at the family home, 51 Harel Battalion St." She knew with some certainty that this address was on a street only partially paved, it was in a newer area on the outskirts of town, a place where there was a long-standing battle between the already defeated orange and grapefruit groves and the developers of already planned neighborhoods. "Mourning are his wife, sister, son, daughter, daughter-in-law, grandchildren." Avigdor was excited about taking her there, he thanked her for remembering him and for considering him close enough to be able to ask for help. They agreed to meet at five in the afternoon, near his car, which was parked in the back lot, and the whole morning before they set out Avigdor cleaned the car with a bucket of water, a long-handled brush, and a rag. He was dressed in an undershirt and shorts; they were comfortable enough to allow his small paunch to spill over the belt which held his hips with an elastic band. In this way he cleaned and dried, polished the outside and vacuumed well on the inside, he did this for a long time and with considerable noise, none of which was lost on Malka's ears.

At exactly the appointed time they met near the old white Subaru, which he had extricated earlier from its spot in the row of cars that faced the small turning-around space, the playground for the children of the building. He was in his white shirt, excited as a young man; she was in a light brown suit and a yellow blouse. On it was a pin in the shape of a leaf. He turned the ignition key, starting the motor, and rolled slowly from the building's parking lot to the street, careful to avoid the soldier who walked on the sidewalk across the car's path. "It's great that you are so careful." She sat with the new small purse that she had bought this morning on her lap, both her hands clasping it on the top. "Wait," he said to her, "we haven't arrived at the highway yet, the main street is still in front of us, and the stoplights, and it's all the way on the other side, behind the market and then to the left, you know." The main street was humming with cars and people gathered at the intersections like sheep at the watering hole, all drawn there by an inexplicable force. Avigdor made his way through it without getting scratched or crushed, and Malka felt particularly confident.

Devorah sat on a wide sofa bed covered in a white sheet that was too small for the sofa. On her right sat an elegant old woman, her silver hair tinged with a glint of green which sparkled from afar, and to her left sat a young man with a few days of growth on his face, a black kippah on his head, and a long, wide, twisted tear in his shirt. A quiet conversation was going on in the spacious room. Six mourners and consolers sat on chairs placed along the walls. Some of the chairs were twins of the table of the orphaned dining room set, which had been pushed aside. On it were bottles of soda and disposable cups. Among the heavy wooden chairs, a few plastic chairs mixed brazenly, brought from someplace else.

As they entered, anonymous and the object of curiosity, they lingered for a few minutes, until Malka recognized Devorah and walked over to her confidently. Each looked at the other, emitting a quiet dirge, shaking their heads in a steadily increasing rhythm, with small gestures of sorrow. And as if on cue they exchanged these thoughts without words: "I know what you are going through, and you know what I'm going through, and when I see you like this–and this too is just the way things are–even when you are in pain you accept your lot as you should, my dear heroine. Now, everyone around you shares in your sorrow; but very soon you'll be alone, and now I too have come to share your pain, and because we understand each other so well, I share your pain a little more than the others, but it's mostly because of you, and not so much because of your dead–that will be your sorrow when you are alone–but my pain will be over your cry, which will come soon, falling out of your mouth when we fall on each other's necks."

Devorah cleared the place next to her for Malka, between her and her son. "Her poor husband was sick too, he was right near Meir, and he saw all of the suffering." And when she sat down she clasped with significance the hand of the bored orphan, and the hand of a man of about seventy who approached and then returned silently to his place. Now they rearranged themselves, investigating, seeking consolation, and sniffing about, until the feeling came over all of them that the new arrangement was fine. A little while later the conversation picked up again, and Devorah conveyed to Malka those few details necessary to understand the connections between everyone there, "except for the one in the pants, him I don't know."

"That's Avigdor," Malka answered, "a very good man, our downstairs neighbor, he's helping us now that Yitzhak is sick." Avigdor nodded in agreement. "He brought me here in his car; you live on the edge of town, and I didn't know... how everything in this area has developed!" Devorah looked at him from a distance. "Really a good guy" she agreed, and offered: "Maybe a little something to drink?"

Through the open door walked a good-looking woman in a black dress and earrings; you could see that she had dressed for the visit. Her hair was set, and she had carefully applied dark lipstick. She held in front of her a platter covered with a paper napkin. On it were two neatly arranged rows of sliced cake. Her entry silenced all conversation between the visitors, until the well-dressed woman hurried and placed her offering in front of the widow–"May the taste of this console you"–and then she turned to the periphery, took a chair from among the plastic ones, and placed it facing Devorah, put her platter on it, and then she brought another chair for herself and sat down next to her offering. "Take some and be strengthened, my good neighbor," she suggested in a voice roughened by years of smoking. Her well-groomed fingernails were covered with reddish-pink polish; the color was different than that of her lipstick, which had been chosen carefully to mark the occasion of mourning. Malka took a piece of cake and broke it in two, biting into one part, "This is good, really excellent," and handed the other half to Avigdor: "Come closer, it's worth it." Avigdor joined the circle, which meant leaving the others who were outside of it, and took the half-piece of cake.

"I'm Nadia, two floors up," she said to Malka and Avigdor. Her smile lingered.

"And I'm Malka," she answered. "How did you make this cake? It's really exceptional!" And to prove her point she bit into the piece of cake again.

A loud gale of laughter came from the kitchen and one voice, less childish than the others, kept going after the others subsided. "It's the grandchildren," Devorah explained, "May they only be healthy, it's very hard for them now that Meir is gone."

Nadia got a lot of satisfaction from the success that had come her way, and she offered a taste of the cake to those sitting outside of their circle of four people. "Please," and she demonstrated "mmm" with her mouth, "delicious ..." Only then did she turn to answer Malka:

"You'd be surprised how simple it is."

"What's that special taste it has?"

"That's from the ginger that I add." Nadia lowered her voice as if transmitting a secret. "I'll tell you how I do it." She sat up, straightening her back. "I take a hundred grams of butter and three quarters of a cup of sugar, blend them together, add two eggs and mix it all up well"– she demonstrated with her right hand–"and then add a tablespoon of lemon peel, and add a teaspoon of lemon juice. But then ..."–she checked to see if people were listening to her–"I add just a drop of ginger to taste, and that really is the whole secret."

"But what's the cake itself made of?" Malka asked.

"It's very simple," she smiled. Avigdor took another piece, and swallowed it. "First I sift together a cup and-a-half, maybe a little more, of flour, with a teaspoon and a half of baking powder, a quarter of a teaspoon of salt, and add it to the cake mix, but what's very important," she lingered, "vvvery ... important"–Devorah tensed and drew closer to the edge of the sofa–"It's important to mix it quickly, and to take a cup of milk, not a whole cup, and add a little of flour and a little milk, each time a little of each, and then to put it in a cake pan, the round kind, with a hole in the middle, and before that oil it well, and add a little flour, so that it doesn't stick." She lifted her palms to the sides and looked at her astonished audience. "And that's the whole secret."

"And how about the baking?" Devorah asked.

"Baking–about a half hour, but not at a high heat."

They got up to go. Avigdor clasped Devorah's outstretched hand for a long time, until her shoulders began to tremble– "And may God console you among the mourners of Zion"– and when he turned to the right he crushed with the sole of his shoe the small cake crumb that fell earlier from Nadia's hand to her dress and then to the floor, and that then continued rolling near his shoe, and when he lifted his shoe from the crumb, no trace was left of it; it had stuck to the sole of his shoe and with it left the house at 51 Harel Brigade St.

An evening chill set in, and a light breeze rustled the tops of the sparse trees of the new neighborhood.

*CHAPTER 9:*

# Cafe Select

*T*wo hours passed and she hadn't shown up and he sat there and realized that she would never arrive, and what was wouldn't be anymore. His past, from the time he grew up until this moment, shrank, got hazy, cracked, and he couldn't remember himself in that past: not being dusted with sawdust in the carpentry shop, nor in Aviva's arms, clean and mechanical, and it wasn't him running like a madman on the ridge of a wooded hill in the fires of Lebanon–running across to Chouf Mountains in the direction of Bhamdoun. He tried to recall the taste of sawdust, licked his lips and sensed the sweetness of the espresso. He was shocked by his haziness, and a slight tremor travelled up from the palms of his hands and his mouth was dry. He spread out his trembling hands in front of him, the hairy backs of them first, and then he turned them over with his palms facing him and he saw the streams gently lapping varieties of trees–groves of cherry trees, maple, and again he turned his palms over–and he saw the thin water channels and the veneer into which they chose to drain–into the creases along the width of his fingers–and the trembling in his hands erased the vision before him. He came back, and with his roughened tongue wiped away the remnants of the taste, and then took a deep breath, filling his chest until it strained his ribs, and they were braked by the thin bamboo netting of his rattan chair, a chair that supported his back up to his shoulders, half the height of his back. A small round cafe table with a brown Formica surface, bent metal frame, and strong black iron legs was between his belly and the rest of the place. You could push against this table without any worries. He grabbed the sides of the table with a strong grip, and then gripped it even harder, until the edges of his fingernails turned blue. Gripping the table cut down the trembling in his palms–they were cold in this foreign autumn–and then the trembling stopped completely. He loosened his grip and the blood flowed back to his extremities like the mad race of a colony of ants.

"Cafe Select," she had said to him, and then she licked his neck until she reached behind his ear. He was pleased that she wasn't turned off by the dandruff in his hair.

"Cafe Select," she repeated, "at two in the afternoon next Tuesday, on the Montparnasse. Wait until twothirty, my train comes in from Toulouse at a quarter to one; get off at the Metro Station at Metro Vavine."

At twenty-five minutes to one he arrived at the Select. He took a cab from the Hotel Royal Saint Germain–three stars, but clean. The cab got stuck in traffic, and at the near corner the driver made a careful U-turn and returned the way he came. Again he passed the hotel, going in the opposite direction. A yellow glass sign, "Hotel," was written in large letters from top to bottom, and in smaller letters, from left to right and in two rows, "Royal" in the first line, and under it, "Saint Germain." They passed in front of the McDonalds in which he had eaten a McChicken just a half hour earlier with a large Coke, and then they turned left at the square across from the Montparnasse tower. They travelled another two hundred meters, and the driver pulled to a stop, smiling. He was embarrassed that he took a cab for only one minute. But then how could he have known that it was so close by? Although when he had asked the agent–Yehezkel's wife–for a hotel, he demanded one near Montparnasse.

The sidewalk of the boulevard was wet from an earlier rain. He went into the tent of the cafe, which sprawled over half the area meant for pedestrians. They had to pull themselves away from the building awnings to the side of the cars. First he sat in the street section, under the rust-colored angled canvas roof. Three large round gas heaters, each with a Chinese-looking metal hat, were hung in the space above the few customers. Though they reminded him of the chicken-coop ovens used on cold nights in his moshav in the Judean Hills, he didn't stay warm, and he entered the old-fashioned cafe. A waiter in jeans and sturdy black shoes brought him the bitter double espresso. The wide door from the tent area to the house opened and closed; the cold from the outside seeped in–first it trickled, and then it was sharp. The music reverberated in the large space, too loud for the middle-aged ambience of the place.

Hagit had told him that in the twenties and thirties the Select was the refuge and meeting place of writers, painters, and poets whose names he couldn't remember; but she could enumerate them to him. It seemed to him that Sartre was among them. He didn't know if he was an actor, a singer, or a painter, but she had used his name a number of times, and that made him important to him.

Now he sat and stared out of the tall windows of the Select. They were framed in old thick dark wood; it was good carpentry work, the kind his father did when he was a kid. He sat and stared out through the large chicken-coop- like tent, where customers were sitting zipped up in their jackets and scarves, their backs to him and their faces looking out beyond the plastic curtain to the boulevard. A large menu board, propped up on an easel, stood with its back to him and blocked out the bottom right side of his view. Most of the traffic on the street, at this afternoon hour on Montparnasse, went to the left and eastward–slowly, bumper to bumper. Traffic toward the city, to the right and westward, was fast and sparse. A Paris municipal bus blocked his view from time to time, letting off pleasant-looking French passengers. A thin white tree, trapped in a green, wide, iron cage, whose bars pointed to the cloudy sky, stood on the Select side of the boulevard. On the other side too, the side of the La Coupole restaurant, four traffic lanes from its companion, stood another captive tree, its bark peeled off and its surface covered with soot. It looked like its brother tree, though from Herzl's distant vantage point it looked thinner. The view was broken by the awning of La Coupole, whose color was bright lipstick-red. Three gold stars competed at the sides of the sign on both sides of the name, whose letters were also in gold. The building across the street was of glass and iron, and those sitting in it were coddled in human warmth. Why did that whore have to pick the Select for him to chill his balls in–why not in La Coupole across the way? What a nasty plot. She never intended to come to their meeting. The cold in the Cafe chilled his nostrils. He despised the waiter, who left the door open, and he didn't know how to tell him to close it. He moved his shoes, socks, and toes in order to thaw them out. The waiter stood with his back to him, staring out through the glass and plastic, and rolling in his fingers a fifty franc note.

A man in a khaki jacket, carrying in his right hand a bicycle wheel and in his left hand a plastic bag–he had closely-cropped black hair combed up from his forehead–stood on the opposite pavement under the gold stars and looked at him, directly into his eyes. He correctly identified him, and when he turned his body he continued looking at him and said something to him.

She sent him to give me a message. He tensed up. He stood up, pushing his table aside. Maybe she took sick, or, God forbid, had an accident and she's lying in a hospital in Toulouse, unconscious. For a moment he regretted cursing her in his heart; the cold he felt was replaced by a choking sensation in his throat. He swallowed his saliva. And why was he carrying a bicycle wheel, and why a goy? And what is this foolishness of sending a messenger?

A bus pulled in from the left and blocked the view of the boulevard. A tall black woman, thin and beautiful, her hair done in tall fashion, got off using the back door slowly and lightly, then floated to the right. "Has she become black?" he wondered for a moment. When the facade of La Coupole was again visible, the messenger was no longer there. He was gone with his bicycle wheel. In the meanwhile the lights of the city came on. He hadn't managed to tell Herzl a word of the message, not an address, not the name of an institution. And how would he have delivered the message? The messenger was a local, and as for himself, he didn't know a word of French.

He noticed that the waiter's order book had a hole in its side, and he sat down slowly, guiding himself with his hands as they caressed and grasped the low bamboo frame of the chair, and in the hole in the corner of the waiter's order book was a metal ring, its circumference a centimeter, and then he sat down and let his hands fall, and in the ring was a chain with small round links, and the chain hung against the man's thigh, and then he closed his eyes, and the chain had slid up to the man's hips, and was caught on his belt, and then calm and quiet settled in on him.

Three hours in this stupid cafe, three hours he's been sitting there, and he's paid no attention to the number of the bus that stops at the station. A dozen buses must have passed and how could he not have seen the number of the bus, written clearly and hung on a metal sign that hangs out on the side, and the sign far enough from the poster so that he can see it: ninety-one. On the ad he saw the face of Denzel Washington. What is a black American doing in Montparnasse? Damn it ...he shrugged his shoulders. He turned toward the hotel. In front of it walked a tall man carrying a plastic bag (and without a bicycle wheel). The man was almost bald and remarkably ugly. The lights of early evening sparkled everywhere, and on the front of the black Montparnasse tower digital messages were broadcast, but these didn't convey to Herzl either a message or any hope, he only saw changing letters and images. Palm trees danced on spotted white clouds, and the image of a green-faced woman wearing red sunglasses shook in the center of the screen, becoming smaller, and then disappearing completely.

He tried to tell himself that from the very beginning there was something about her–about Hagit–something vague, and even, it just might be, something unstable, though always fascinating. He caught himself thinking about her in the past tense, and he felt his chin tremble. She wasn't a child, though she looked younger than her age. An elderly father, that's what she told him, lived in Haifa, distant and disapproving, and a wealthy mother–who had married again in Germany–was the person closest to her. Now it seemed strange to him that she had begun studying medicine in Germany, studied for two and a half years, lived with her mother, and then left, came back to Israel to an empty house and signed up to study social work, and this too she never completed, and she acts self-important, like a doctor, but in reality works as a paramedic in the evening shift in the emergency room. For a moment it seemed to him as if she was waving at him from a car at the intersection of Montparnasse and the Rue des Rennes. He waved and hurried on, but when he got closer she broke off and drove away. "I should have been more careful," he thought. "Idiot," he whispered; "what a fool," he cried; "jerk!" he yelled at his image in the show window of a sweet-shop, and those passing him on the street remained deaf and indifferent to his voice, and suddenly he regretted that he had thought badly of Hagit–hadn't he himself missed in his stupidity the messenger, carrying the wheel, that she sent him from afar?

He passed in front of his hotel on Rue de Rennes and walked on the street lit up with the light of shop windows. The streets intersected the Rue de Rennes at an angle, and he had to be careful at the corner of Raspail, to see where the traffic was coming from and where it was going, so that he didn't get hurt by the wheels of those who were speeding. When he got to the corner of Boulevard St. Germain, as soon as he turned the corner, the earth opened up and threatened to swallow him. The stones of the sidewalk lifted up and cracked, as if a violent hammer had hit them from below, and blocks of black twisted pipes burst from the belly of the earth and pointed jaggedly at the sky. People walked by, avoiding the entrance to hell, and went on their way, as if nothing had happened. A slight vapor rose from the spot and it was as if light from the table lamps of the angels of hell sharpened the metal fingers of the wounded earth. He went closer and saw that a primeval ocean was boiling in the depths of the pit. Getting even closer and bending on his knees he was drawn into the depths, and he lay flat on the twisted sidewalk, shoved his right hand into that lake of hell, and when he couldn't reach it he put out his other hand and crawled into the mouth of the volcano. He went on pushing and crawling, shoving the sidewalk blocks of Paris with his knees and elbows, his right shoulder and arm stretched out downward, drawn in, sinking into the deep until he touched it.

The waters of the pool were dark and shallow. Not hot, not a lake, not an ocean ... "What is this supposed to be?" he wondered. He tried to get the whole picture but could only grasp details. He felt for the walls and slapped the water, which sprayed his face. Only when he closed his eyes could he make things out. "It's an environmental urban art installation," is no doubt how Aviva would have explained it, and electric spotlights flashed at him from the bottom of the pool.

"The whole thing is a meter and a half deep." He laughed and sat up straight in the water, fully clothed. The water reached to his hips. Yes, his face, neck, and shoulders got wet when he fell in head first and his legs were pulled in next, but when he sat up in the cold water his tongue was dry and his lips burned with thirst. Then he bent over and drank with an open mouth, and the legs of the passersby were at the level of his eyes. Only one pair of brown leather shoes, with a set of short women's heels, took an interest in his lonely situation, and a wonderful pair of perfect legs rose up from them, sheathed in grey nylon stockings, they went up and up, until the blinding light of the street lamp.

In the police station of the Latin Quarter they put a blanket on him to cut down his shivering. He remembered a heavy hand on his shoulder, and remembered that that night he didn't sleep in the hotel, nor the day after, and that the mattress that night was hard under him but wide, and it was very quiet there. He saw that the walls of his room were plastered and that the short lace curtain was shorter than the window, which looked out on the undressed brick wall of the building across the way. On the wall of the room was a calendar from an organization that gives assistance to starving children. A child with the face of an aging Indian was grasping with both of his small palms an outstretched hand. For a whole day Herzl alternated between sleeping and staring at the picture, and in the afternoon, late, he thought of Guy and how he blew his nose with such seriousness, folded the wet tissue twice and put it in his pants pocket.

The detective who spoke with him before he left him alone addressed him in French, and then in an English he couldn't understand. The detective wrote on the forms in front of him and then gave them to him to sign. His cheeks were smooth, like those of someone who had never shaved, but lines radiated from his eyes, forehead and mouth, and the lines created by his smile reminded him of the face of an Israeli television entertainer, whose face now arose before him. What's his name? Dammit! When he went out into the street, alone in the big city, he remembered, yes, Moni Moshonov, and burst out laughing, leaning against the corner of a house, laughing to himself. At the corner of the street he stopped at a kiosk and bought a map of the city, checked the street sign and the sign above the corner and immediately found where he was on the map, drew an imaginary line, and went to his hotel. He went up to his room in the elevator–maximum weight no more than three people–and brushed his teeth. He shaved and went into the shower, stood in the hot water until the pads of his fingers got soft, shampooed his hair, and then did it again, as usual. He jumped into the bed naked, landed on his belly, turned over on his back, pressed the remote, changed channels, three, and stopped at CNN.

The next morning he walked to the Select and remembered the way, like a pro. The neon cafe sign was still lit up from afar, as if they had forgotten to turn it off since that evening when they hadn't met. When he approached from west to east he noticed the word "Atelier," written, in not especially prominent and fading letters on rough material made out of brown canvas. The clear plastic covering was swept up out of the way and he saw three young people talking over their early beers in an inside room. "Atelier" was also written on the menu board at the entrance, and also inside. "Atelier, that's an artist's studio," he said out loud to himself. He massaged his temples and kept walking on the avenue, but only a little farther, and next door, shoulder to shoulder to it, sat the Select, calm, bright and clear, decorated with its glass windows, and hiding itself in waves of starched-looking greenish curtains. They were hanging along the whole facade facing the street, hanging on rings of that same fabric, rings three fingers wide, and they hung from a gold-colored railing that reached from the height of his thigh to the tiles on the floor. When he stepped into the cafe he realized that they each might have waited while at no distance at all from each other, and even though he regretted it, he was also very happy.

A waiter, zipped into a white suit, moved a white straw chair so that he could sit. "Bonjour, monsieur," he said as he wiped the surface of the table with a practiced gesture and brought an ashtray and menu closer to him.

CHAPTER 10:

# Heather

*H*erzl returned to Israel twelve days after Malka disappeared. In the airport he found only a few leftover shekels in his pocket, and he knew he wouldn't be able to take a taxi to his parents' house. His credit card was blocked, this he knew in Paris–"Speak to your bank in Israel; it's an order from there it seems." This in serious tones, from an older female bank clerk in a branch near the Place Bastille. He tried to free one hundred shekels from the airport ATM, and here too, in his own country, in his own language, it didn't work.

Two buses, a hot sweaty afternoon, the second one crowded with wage slaves from the suburbs–a trip of more than two hours–including a layover in the Tel Aviv Central Bus Station. "They only discovered that she disappeared three days after she didn't come back from the market," said Heather, after they finished the supper she had prepared for them. She had put out fragile utensils of glass and silver, things he didn't know existed in his childhood home. "You won't believe what I found in the kitchen cabinets," she said proudly, and for each item on the menu she put out a separate utensil. Even the bread, in two thin crisp slices–white and airy–she placed in a silver candy bowl, on a round embroidered napkin. When she smiled he noticed delicate lines radiating from the corners of her eyes. A fair, shining child, and in her hands holiday utensils, and they transmit happiness to Heather; but to him they neither added nor detracted–they were only fragments of sadness. And yet this is his house, there is no doubt about it, the home of his childhood, youth, and adolescence. The walls hold on to that same washable wallpaper, and the postcard is there too, from the trip to Cyprus in a frame that's faded over the years, hung on a nail that he banged into the wall with obvious pride. How many years had passed since the day his mother asked him to "bang into the wall for me a meter from the tile"? If he were to move the picture, a square of the wallpaper's original color would be uncovered, protected like the skin of Aviva, when she takes off, at summer's end, the bra of the bathing suit, and her breasts–confident, directly from the sea–are brighter than the rest of her. But the wind, and the smell, and the woman who today filled the house and the kitchen, they were different.

On mornings that she was sick, when she was lying around in enforced solitude, the young Heather had to provide explanations to her mother, excuses that couldn't be questioned–excuses that were serious and most precise–as distinct from those simple answers she gave when cutting school. And when the family said grace, before they ate, when they bent their heads and closed their eyes, she felt true gratitude to the household gods for the dishes, for their tastes and variety, for their texture and smell. When she grew up, this feeling of thanks extended to the most comfortable and sophisticated of Tel Aviv's restaurants. Jonathan was wrong when he connected Heather's excitement when they ate–and her self-reflection and absorption when the meal was over, then she was withdrawn and silent–to himself and her love for him.

"Money, a home, wisdom, beauty, even a happy family–all these are a matter of luck–but bread and water are God's; they are a measure of reward and punishment." Father Trevor, in his sermons before his flock, provided her for as long as she could remember with an escape from the discipline of home life.

"Anyone who dies of sloppy eating"–and here he was alluding to Troy, her classmate, fat and red-nosed, who choked to death in a steak-eating contest at the new diner, and was resuscitated afterward in the ambulance, on the way to the hospital but was brain-damaged, stuck in a wheelchair and without consciousness–"God struck him down, like someone hit by lightning in the field, lightning that came down like fire from heaven to earth, and found its victim from among all the beasts of the field and all people."

"Anyone who gives thanks for food won't choke over it," her mother promised every time they saw Troy on the main street, pushed in a wheelchair by his sister. Heather believed her mother, not only because of the respect that Father Trevor had for her, but also because of her love for her. From her Aunt Tricia, who chose the life of a nun, she kept her distance. Later she came to understand that God could be found in her own kitchen and her own pots, and not necessarily in the prayers of strangers, with which Heather had nothing to do.

At the first Passover Seder in his home, Yitzhak made sure that they didn't read "Pour out thy wrath on the nations." He also chose for her a special Haggadah, with English translation, one sold by the Jerusalem Orphans' Home, and made sure that Yuval, his sister's son, who was a sailor and an expert in the English of sailors and whores, would sit next to her and translate for her the Jewish grace after meals.

Afterward she photocopied in the street the translation of the grace, from that same Haggadah of the Jerusalem Orphans' Home, and sent it to her mother and father in Oklahoma, so they'd understand, and maybe that way it would be easier for them. She had heard disappointment and reservation in their voices from the day that they made their decision. Before that, when he was courting her, Jonathan felt comfortable with the family in the farming town a two-hour drive from Oklahoma City, and it was easy to connect with her father and brothers when they went to the baseball park. Heather never stopped explaining her conversion to Judaism, which was part of the whirlwind of falling in love. She was positive that her identity hadn't been damaged. According to her, Shifra, the college rabbi, was just a good friend of hers, and the marriage to Jonathan–just part of their experience as a couple. She tended to underplay the importance of her marriage; anything to play down the rift that she had left behind her. "God doesn't get in between people, He's very busy, generally, but for reasons best known to Him, he takes an interest in the life of Aunt Tricia, and not in mine." In New York it was easier. In the big city Heather found more than a few Jewish-Christian women, until she was able to sniff them out with a special sense of smell that she developed. Jonathan picked out a profession for her when they went back to Israel, "a scout for Christian women who are standing in line at the Ministry of the Interior to get their identity papers."

The children were born quickly, to protect themselves and give them stability. Only Yitzhak was able to open her eyes to realize that she had done an injustice to her parents, and that there was no making up for it. From what he said she also learned that Malka stopped being happy from the day they got married. "But as for me, you came to me as a daughter," he revealed to her. You came to me in place of mine, the one that left us and apostatized in the craziness of making Teshuvah." When he spoke of the apostate he always sighed, "She abandoned the commandment, the essence of the revelation at Sinai, honor your father and mother, the one that involves a reward for its observance: So that your days might be lengthened–she abandoned it and followed the mission of the rabbis." Yitzhak promised Heather that the grandchildren that he would have through her would be kosher Jewish children, even though her conversion was Reform. "The girls were switched for me twenty years too late," he complained.

It was impossible for Heather not to love Aviva. The phone conversations between them, since their honeymoon visit to Israel, were an increasing part of their monthly expenses. Jonathan used to surprise her from the back and kiss her on the neck. He also did this every time he saw the bill that came from AT&T; its details told of the women's friendship, growing out of choice. "You won me over," Aviva said to her once, "at your Thanksgiving dinner, when Guy sat on your knee, and you sang holiday songs to him, and I counted four times that you wiped the kid's impossible snot on the table cloth." Heather didn't remember that occasion at all. "Israeli imagination" she called the legend Aviva had woven about her. Malka hated the story, and complained to Herzl, "Your Aviva has also drafted the gentile against me."

"Twice we got in touch and talked to Dad," she said with emotion, "You know I call every Friday, when you're eating here, all together, and it took a long time for Yitzhak to answer the second time I called. It was clear that he had been alone at home for a couple of days." From her story it was clear that she got in touch with Aviva and didn't hear anything in her voice that conveyed worry or tension, but she understood that Herzl was out of the country, which was unusual for him, and that Aviva wasn't interested in explaining her husband's trip, or in searching for Malka—but when she begged her, Aviva agreed to find out. On her visit the following day, Aviva found Yitzhak alone and too confused to understand where Malka was. The dirty dishes and the empty food packaging that was strewn about the kitchen counter, the sink, and the refrigerator, indicated three or four days of neglect. Empty cans of peas, beans, and pineapple filled the garbage can under the sink to its brim. She didn't understand why Yitzhak made sure to throw these cans in the garbage can, while the rest of the trash was left where it was when it was useful; it wasn't thrown out when used up. Yitzhak was shaved and washed, his shirt was a Shabbat shirt, but his pants–pajama pants that were soiled with hardened spit-up. Clothes and sheets that had been changed were thrown in the bathtub. In the shower that was dripping when Aviva entered stood a wooden chair that was missing from the kitchen; a little pool of water was on its seat. "She went out to the market to shop with an overnight bag she took down from the closet in the bedroom," Yitzhak said, "and she showed me where the cans of food were that she bought especially for me. And also," he went on without emotion, "she asked me not to worry, and not to bother the children, because she has something important to take care of." And with pride he added, "And I'm really not wanting for anything."

Twice a day Heather talked on the phone to Yitzhak, until she bought an airline ticket on El Al, at the counter in the airport in New York. Jonathan claimed that she was exaggerating, but was happy that she took the responsibility instead of him, especially during the week he was so busy with the annual report of the limited liability project of which he was so proud. Aviva picked Heather up at the airport and let her go up the stairs alone, carrying a small travel bag. With obvious joy she handed over the keys to Malka's house. "I was so sure that you would come, of all of them only you, only you are my daughter." Yitzhak welcomed her without surprise, even though it was Salim, the veteran Arab carpentry worker, who opened the door, after she rang the doorbell twice–the second ring longer than the first–and saw Salim's shadow darken the peephole in the door. He stared at her for a long time. "Excuse me for checking, I'm here without a permit," he explained, and she accepted his apology with a hug, her bag waving at his shoulder, "I know you, I'm Jonathan's wife," and the teapot spread its steam over the sink. Yitzhak stood, thinner than she remembered, behind Salim and mumbled, "A blessing on your head, a blessing on you." He insisted that with his very own hands he'd make her the lemon tea she loved; the tea bags were kept in the house for her increasingly infrequent visits. "You forgot my brown sugar," she was almost insulted.

It was two days now that she had been with him, scrubbing, washing, cooking vegetable soup and fried pieces of chicken breast, and she aired out the rooms and let the light in, until they were blinded by sunlight, sunlight that they hadn't remembered for years–on the walls and on the surprised pieces of furniture. On the kitchen table and on Yitzhak's night table colorful fresh poppies peeked out of Malka's collection of clear glass vases; they had been liberated from the kitchen. "Yesterday Aviva was here and the four of us ate together," she said in her heavy American accent. "She brought pizza on the way, after work."

"Four?" Yizhak wondered, "Jonathan also arrived?"

"You are simply an asshole, that's what you are." Heather was enraged, and he saw real anger in her eyes, even though–as was her habit–she spoke in that quiet tone that you had to be wary of.

"No, idiot, not Jonathan, it was your son Guy who was here, he too eats once in a while, if you don't mind."

"I care, what do you mean? Of course I care," he apologized in an odd voice.

"Look, it's your business, I'm on the outside and don't get involved." She sat down across from him. He tried to answer, and she motioned with her hand for him to be quiet. "We've been together for three hours, talking, that's O.K. with me, but your father is alone in the living room, and you haven't gotten in touch to let people know you've returned–and I'm not getting involved."

"Tell me, don't you care where I've been?" He spoke like a hurt child. "You didn't ask."

"Please don't tell me, I don't want to know, let's go and sit with your father." She smiled at him and got up, ruffled his hair with one finger and lingered while kissing his head–he began to feel jealous of his brother Jonathan. She went out without him, and he heard her say in her light tone, "Did you fall asleep again watching television, Dad?'

The evening passed in an uneasy silence. A fat comedian giggled and scratched his way across the flickering screen, and no one, except for the anonymous crowd inside the box, responded to his efforts. Yitzhak signaled to Herzl that he should sit next to him, and between short naps he felt for Yitzhak's hand and squeezed it until he dozed off again, his chin falling on his chest, and this allowed Herzl to withdraw his hand in embarrassment to his lap. Heather called Jonathan collect after the TV program "Mabat." He heard them chattering for a long time–about stuff going on there, and about Salim's visit, and his own name was mentioned once, and at the end "kisses, love you," Hebrew mixed up with English, and she didn't call Herzl to talk to his brother, and then the phone receiver was clicked into its cradle.

The following afternoon Dr. Sovrin and the lawyer Brinker came to visit. Brinker's hair had some grey in it; they hadn't met with him since the meeting in which Yitzhak and Herzl arranged the details of family ownership of the carpentry shop. "Your father invited us for a conversation," the doctor announced. Yitzhak insisted that Heather get his clothes ready for this quite secular morning, "As if I was going today to the synagogue, and also shined shoes, if it's not difficult for you." Washed, shaved, and well-combed, long before the time of the appointment, he sat in the living room, master of his house, his face looking the way it used to look. Herzl felt that he was losing control over his life. Heather had gone out shopping at least two hours ago, and he was a stranger, and empty, in his father's house. He still didn't have it in him to get in touch with Aviva, and he remembered that he hadn't left this house since he arrived. He stood, embarrassed, at the entrance, when Brinker and Dr. Sovrin came in. "This way, madame, this way, sir, this way please," Yitzhak called out from his distant chair. "Close the door, please," Yitzhak asked the lawyer.

He heard them greeting each other on the other side of the milky glass of the door, and here he was alone in his own house. He went out to the steps and sat, barefoot, on the top step. The house door moved with the gentle breeze and shut behind him. He noticed that he was wearing gym shorts and a T-shirt. The chill of the stone rose up through the soles of his feet.

After an eternity the door was opened. Yitzhak opened it himself and the guests came out, Sovrin first. "You don't have to take all of this so hard, Herzl (she pronounced it Hartzl). Your father did this with a clear mind, and considering what happened last month, he did the right thing." To Herzl she sounded patronizing, arrogant, and chastising. "There's a copy of the summary on the table for you." They left like strangers, not connected to each other, the doctor hurrying along, and they didn't look back, even when they reached the landing at the end of the first set of stairs. Herzl remained sitting half a floor above Brinker's bald spot, and the two turned around, facing him, busy with their exit, and they didn't notice him, and then they disappeared from sight, and only the sounds of Brinker's cough and Sovrin's heels could be heard as they diminished on the way down the street.

"Why are you sitting like that?" His father leaned against the door and Herzl heard his own blood rise in his chest and up the sides of his neck to his ear lobes–and didn't answer. Yitzhak grabbed his son by the shoulder of his undershirt and shook some sense into him until he agreed to get up. He stood facing his father and they looked at each other, Yitzhak smiling and shy and Herzl worried, searching his father's face. They stood that way, and quietly the sinuous sound of a Middle Eastern melody drifted in from one of the apartments, until Herzl fell on Yitzhak's neck, sobbing, and Yitzhak patted him on his back, trying hard to maintain his balance, until he held onto the railing and stabilized himself. "Enough, son, enough for you, I no longer have the strength to take care of you, now it's your turn to take care of me and your mother, she too is no longer made of steel." Herzl quieted down, straightened up and stared, embarrassed, at his father, his chastiser. "Now read what I prepared with the lawyer." He pointed toward the living room and turned to the bedroom. "This is too much for one day, I'm going to sleep." Herzl ambled off silently after Yitzhak. "And call your wife and your son, please, now!" Even though Yitzhak was aggressive, his voice cracked.

The agreement–its copies new, its pages stuck together and its corners ironed out as if they had been through a press, stared at Herzl from the low serving table. One copy said "Jonathan and Heather," the one under it said "Herzl." He threw himself into the easy chair reserved for Malka's breakfasts, propped himself up with its wide armrests and pressed his back into the soft back support. He placed the two groups of papers one next to the other and covered both of them with his large hands. He read both of them, one after the other, first the opening sentence, then the last on the page, which was cut off in the middle, and then the last word that was in both copies: "on his behalf." After that he reviewed them, shuffling through both of them, and found that the last word on the second page was "equal," and on the third–"his death." He got up from his place and rushed to the bathroom. He had a powerful urge to piss; it grabbed him and stroked the lower parts of his belly.

He considered the agreement for a while and then picked up the pages with his name on them and read them in sequence, one after the other. Three were handwritten clearly and the fourth, half of which was typed, had at its end, "the undersigned," "the officiating," and at the very bottom of the page, in her handwriting, "witness to the signing, and certifying the clarity of mind of the undersigned, Dr. Sovrin." It was clear now that the document had been prepared a few days before he returned to Israel, and that the details of the decision and its legal formulation had undergone careful consideration. Yitzhak leaves half of his property "to his beloved wife Malka," including half of the apartment and the carpentry shop, and of the kiosk on Weizmann Street, of which Herzl knew nothing. The other half Yitzhak deposits in the hands of the attorney Brinker, who from this point on has power of attorney to act on his behalf, in order that he put the property in one of the mortgage banks. The value of the mortgage will be deposited in a bank account, and it will be used to pay for Yitzhak's stay and care in a senior care facility "that will be found appropriate to his comfort and needs for all the days of his life until the day of his death, including burial expenses and a marble monument." At Yitzhak's death anything left of the deposited money will be divided into four equal parts: one for Herzl, the second for his sister, who "apostatized to orthodoxy"–it said this explicitly in print, the stubborn guy! Herzl smiled to himself–the third to Jonathan and the fourth to Heather. And it also noted that "in the event that one of the above-mentioned dies before the division of the property, his rights will go in equal parts to their descendants." He folded the document carefully and put it in the dresser drawer. Yitzhak slept in his bed the sleep of the righteous, supine and with his shoes still on.

Heather got in touch at ten past six in the evening and asked that he wash up and dress nicely. "You stink from a mile away," she told him, "and it's about time you knew. I'm arriving with important guests at seven-thirty." When she arrived with her guests, Herzl was still in the shower, shampoo lathered in his hair and his eyes closed. He rinsed himself quickly and heard sounds of conversation and laughter in the house. He opened the shower door wide, dripping streams of water onto the bathroom floor. Aviva stood leaning against the porcelain tiles, looking at his nakedness with frank lust. He grabbed her in a powerful clutch, like back in the beginning, dripping water into her clothes and her face, and in their assault on each other's lips, breathing heavily and groaning, they didn't manage at first to put tongue to tongue, until he caught her cheeks in his palms. He licked the tears that rolled down her cheeks and saw Guy standing in the doorway and staring, amazed at his parents. Heather stood in back of him, hands on his shoulders and her chin on his head. Aviva came to first, grabbing a towel from the old robe hanger. "Take it, Herzl, cover up." Only then did he realize that his erection was powerful and apparent. "Thanks." He took it slowly and wrapped it around his waist. "Come, Guy," Aviva called. "Give your father a kiss for returning to us safely."

The dinner that Heather ordered was pizza with olives. The delivery man told them, in that indifferent weak tone reserved for experienced delivery men, "this week there's a deal, anyone ordering a big one with extras gets a container of Cola as a gift." Guy found in this bottle of Coke a reason to be happy and announced: "I asked for it first," and meeting no resistance, he adopted it as his own and sat down next to Herzl, waving his triumph at his father–"I've got it, I've got it." Before the deliveryman had arrived Guy wove a web of silvery strands made out of a tremor of sadness, and he caught in that web the walls, the furniture, and the people, the atmosphere of happiness of the family reunion. "I don't want to give him a kiss," and later, "Bad daddy, let him bring Grandma home first."

The pizza shortened the long silences around the table. "For me without olives" (Guy), "Give me his olives" (Herzl), "And for me a thin, little, little one," (Yitzhak). And also "without the crust" and also "only in the middle, where it's soft." Aviva divided it up until the tray was almost empty.

"Look, there's nothing left for you," Heather worried, and she returned a corner of a triangular piece that was bitten into. "That's O.K., sweetie," Aviva's eyelashes fluttered, "I really like the crumbs, I collect them and bring them together with my finger and push them till they stick and eat them by myself, even alone, after they've all left, and I like it that way," she laughed, and didn't lift her eyes to see if they were listening to her. And while she was doing it and explaining and demonstrating, and the thin field of cardboard was cleaned off, Yitzhak got up slowly, pushed with a dragging noise the old wooden chair and dragged his slippers to the toilet, and with the door open, his back to the diners, he pissed hesitantly, stopping and starting again–streams that were suddenly cut off and got stronger until they were one stream.

# CHAPTER 11 :

# Silence

"*I* made it without sugar," Malka said, putting the pale glass of tea in front of Devorah, "and it's not strong; it's the way you like it." It was a thin transparent glass cup without handles, under it a saucer too deep for the cup–it too was transparent–and in the tea a slice of lemon floated, its body immersed, its head clinging to the side of the glass at the point that Malka had sliced it.

"You know, Malka, these new knitting needles are particularly good." She lifted the needles a bit; red woolen knitting was hanging from them as they nuzzled up against each other. "These needles are just the right weight for my hands ..." Her voice was loud and clear, each word separated from its companion and given the appropriate tone. The ball of wool rolled onto the fabric of her dress and from there onto her thighs. Her back was straight, she wasn't leaning back, her arms were lifted a bit, the elbows apart and free from her hips. "Look, Malka," she said as she continued knitting, "your embroidery is sitting here on the table; you haven't even touched it. Why are you hurrying? Come here and sit with me a little."

The TV was on without the sound, it was that way every evening they met, four times a week now, during the winter and the beginning of spring since Devorah had become a widow. She had said, "I only want to see the news," and Malka, though she was used to watching religiously, agreed. "For me, the important thing is that it is on, but if it's that important to you, we can keep the sound off." They agreed that "for a long time there's been' nothing worth listening to." On the TV screen two young comedians were running around; they were woefully skinny, and their hair was cropped so closely you could see their scalps. They were so eager to be heard, but to no avail. The shorter of the two smiled even when he was silent; his partner looked cynical and so sad–he couldn't be cheered up.

"Did you see that they took down Zelinger's old building?"

"No, I didn't. But I heard that the Egged clerk had a heart attack."

"What does he look like?"

"He's tall, with glasses that have thick frames." She signified his height with her hand over her head. "He's friendly. I asked the driver, and he told me." She paused and said, "He isn't really that old."

They sat and worked, each on her own project. From time to time Devorah lifted up her work to see how it was progressing, and each time she did this she stole a glance to see if Malka had noticed how the back of the sweater was turning out, but no, Malka had stuck her needle into the middle of the embroidery, or she showed interest in what was happening on the silent screen, or she had moved to make herself more comfortable on the sofa.

"I made some apple compote for Yitzhak, and tomorrow I'll bring it to the rest home–so he'll get better." Malka was planning out loud, pursing her lips. "Mmmm ... so good, I wanted to finish it all myself ..." She moved her tongue quickly from left to right. "I left you some to taste; it's in the jar. Take some home."

"I no longer have anyone to cook for," said Devorah with the hint of a smile.

"You won't believe it, but my daughter-in-law comes over to learn to cook what my son likes to eat; pretty soon the grandson has a bar mitzvah–so she remembered to learn." She wagged her head. Now they are going for counseling, seeing a woman therapist." She put her needlework down and her look demanded full attention to what she was saying. "Once it was yelling and then kisses"–she puckered her mouth to demonstrate a kiss–"that's how we made kids." She put the palm of her hand on her belly. "Today, it's long silences and thoughts, and then you see a therapist. That's the style today, and kids–they're made in test tubes."

"You have nothing to complain about," said Devorah with a smile. "You're exaggerating about your kids, if you'll excuse me, and don't butt in! In my family the oldest girl hasn't gotten married and in yours everyone is pretty well set up." She turned serious: "You know, I wish I had some pleasure from my daughter, even if it's from a test tube. I don't care anymore."

"Look at Salim, our Arab laborer, every year a new kid–he should only be healthy, he doesn't count them anymore, and he makes his whole living from our carpentry shop." Malka didn't want to hear any more about the unmarried daughter.

Devorah put down the knitting needles. "You've been very fortunate with him, that that Arab stayed with Yitzhak when you went to search for Herzl, your delicate son, in Eilat." She brought the cup of tea closer to the edge of the table. "It's cold already."

"This is the second time that you have called him 'delicate.' He should be called 'a saint,' not 'delicate,' because he really is a saint to live the way he does." She checked to see if she was understood, but didn't see in Devorah's face that she had been convinced. "Did you see the new coat he bought this winter, how it suits him?"

"I saw, it really suits him, he's tall, everything suits him, that's how it is when you're tall."

"You know, in Eilat, when I was looking for him, for Herzl, I ate in a restaurant run by Indians, a real one, with all the spices, Avigdor knows the electrician there." She was wrapped up in her memories, "It's hard to believe the tastes and the smells that the Indians eat today."

"What do you mean 'today'? The Indians have had these spices for a thousand years, they've been eating them in peace all that time–very quietly and peacefully, at the same time that the goyim were putting us in the ghetto and slaughtering us Jews." She swayed like a mourner until the topic was forgotten. "You know that I've never been to Eilat, in all these years in Israel." She straightened her arms out. "Do me a favor, check the sweater back that I've finished, how does it look?" She smiled for a while: "Malkale, nu, turn the TV off for me now."

"Fine, I'm turning it off, but first finish the tea; pretty soon we'll have to pour it out." Malka took the cup and brought it closer to Devorah. "Here, take."

"In an hour you'll be getting your grandchild, Guy, right? Today's Thursday, he gets his tutoring." She pointed with her finger to the clunky living room table. "Why doesn't he study in the kitchen, for example? That would be much easier, and ..." She straightened up, elongating her neck, "... healthy for the back. Don't forget he's big now."

"Really, it's good you're letting me know that my grandson is getting big. Thanks a lot."

"Stop with the insults. Since Yitzhak went to the old-age home you've become very touchy," Devorah complained. "Excuse me for interfering again, but it's been three months since Yitzhak left. Doesn't he want to visit on Shabbat? At least to eat with the family?" And she added, "If you'd like me to help with the cooking–whatever you ask."

Malka got up, stood on her bare left foot, stretched out the sole of her right foot in front of her while tilting her back for balance, and wiggled her toes as if to free them from a bothersome cramp. "I have to show you something, Devorah. I bought an electric tub that gives the soles of the feet a jacuzzi. I got it through the mail, you get it in the credit card ads." She took a few steps and returned with a sparkle in her eye. "While I'm getting water, take your shoes off. As a widow you deserve a bit of pampering."

Devorah put down the cup of tea and bent over to take off her shoes.